THE

BEAUTIFUL THINGS

THAT

HEAVEN BEARS

RIVERHEAD BOOKS

a member of Penguin Group (USA) Inc. · New York

2007

THE

BEAUTIFUL THINGS

THAT

HEAVEN BEARS

DINAW MENGESTU

RIVERHEAD BOOKS
Published by the Penguin Group
Penguin Group (USA) Inc., 375 Hudson Street, New York, New York 10014, USA • Penguin
Group (Canada), 90 Eglinton Avenue East, Suite 700, Toronto, Ontario M4P 2Y3, Canada
(a division of Pearson Penguin Canada Inc.) • Penguin Books Ltd, 80 Strand, London
WC2R 0RL, England • Penguin Ireland, 25 St Stephen's Green, Dublin 2, Ireland (a division
of Penguin Books Ltd) • Penguin Group (Australia), 250 Camberwell Road, Camberwell,
Victoria 3124, Australia (a division of Pearson Australia Group Pty Ltd) • Penguin Books
India Pvt Ltd, 11 Community Centre, Panchsheel Park, New Delhi–110 017, India •
Penguin Group (NZ), 67 Apollo Drive, Mairangi Bay, Auckland 1311, New Zealand
(a division of Pearson New Zealand Ltd) • Penguin Books (South Africa) (Pty) Ltd,
24 Sturdee Avenue, Rosebank, Johannesburg 2196, South Africa

Penguin Books Ltd, Registered Offices:
80 Strand, London WC2R 0RL, England

Library of Congress Cataloging-in-Publication Data

Mengestu, Dinaw, date.
The beautiful things that heaven bears / Dinaw Mengestu.
p.   cm.
ISBN-13: 978-1-59448-940-2   ISBN-10: 1-59448-940-8
1. Ethiopians—United States—Fiction. 2. Washington (D.C.)—Fiction.
[1. Race relations—Fiction.] I. Title.
PS3613.E487B43   2007   2006025058
813'.6—dc22

Printed in the United States of America
1   3   5   7   9   10   8   6   4   2

BOOK DESIGN BY AMANDA DEWEY

To Hirut and Tesfaye Mengestu, for everything

ACKNOWLEDGMENTS

To my family for all of their support and for sharing their lives with me, especially Fekada Stephanos, Berhane Stephanos, Zewditu Abebe, Aster Stephanos; to my sister, Bezawit; to my early readers, Manuel Gonzales, Marcela Valdes, Mark Binelli, Benjamin Lytal, Samita Sinha, Jaime Manrique, Mako Yoshikawa, Carin Besser, Alice Quinn, Rattawut Lapcharoensap; to Clarissa Jones, for having made this story possible; to Aamer Madhani and Jonathan Ringen for years of unfailing support; to Meghann Curtis, for listening; to Norma Tilden, for her early guidance; to the New York Foundation for the Arts; to my wonderful agent, PJ Mark, for believing in this book from the very beginning; to my editor, Megan Lynch, for her patience, trust, and most important, for making this a better book; to my uncle, Shibrew; to my grandfather Stephanos.

THE

BEAUTIfUL THINGS

THAT

HEAVEN BEARS

I

At eight o'clock Joseph and Kenneth come into the store. They come almost every Tuesday. It's become a routine among the three of us without our ever having acknowledged it as such. Sometimes only one of them comes. Sometimes neither of them. No questions are asked because nothing is expected. Seventeen years ago we were all new immigrants working as valets at the Capitol Hotel. According to the plaque outside the main entrance, the hotel was built to resemble the Medicis' family house in Italy. On weekends tourists lined the rooftop to stare at the snipers perched on the White House roof. It was there that Kenneth became Ken the Kenyan and Joseph, Joe from the Congo. I was skinnier then than I am now, and as our manager said, I didn't need a nickname to remind him I was Ethiopian.

"You close the store early today?" Kenneth asks, as he walks in and glances at the empty aisles. He comes straight from his job, his suit coat still on despite the early May heat. His shirt is neatly pressed, and his tie is firmly fastened around his neck. Kenneth is an engineer who tries not to look like one. He believes in the power of a well-tailored suit to command the attention and respect of those who might not otherwise give him a second thought. Every week he says the same thing when he walks in. He knows there's no humor in it, but he's come to believe that American men are so successful because they say the same thing over and over again.

"Don't take it from me," he said in his defense once. "Listen to them. Every day. The same thing. Every day my boss comes in, and he says to me, 'You still fighting the good fight Kenneth?' And I put my fist in the air and say, 'Still fighting.' And he says, 'That's what I like to hear.' He makes ninety thousand a year. Ninety thousand. So, I say, 'You close the store early today?' And you say, 'Fuck you.'"

"Fuck you, Ken," I say as the door closes behind him. He smiles gratefully at me whenever I say that. As much as Kenneth has ever needed anything in his life, he has needed order and pre-dictability, small daily reassurances that the world is what it is, regardless of how flawed that may be. He has a small mouth, with full lips that would be considered beautiful on a woman, but that on him come off as overly puckered. He's self-conscious about his teeth, which are slightly brown and bent in the same direction. Joseph pressed him once into saying why, even now with all that he earns, he has never had them fixed. Kenneth smiled a full, wide smile for us before he responded. When he speaks in front of strangers he buries his mouth behind his hand. He rubs his lower lip between his thumb and forefinger, making everything he is embarrassed about disappear.

"You can never forget where you came from if you have teeth

as ugly as these," he said. He grinned once more. He tapped a slightly brown front tooth for effect.

Kenneth looks Kenyan. His skin is dark, his nose is long and thin, and yet his features are soft, almost delicate, like a child's. He's six feet tall, but it's only in the past two years, since he got his job, that's he's ever weighed more than a hundred and fifty pounds. When he's drunk he lifts up his shirt, blows out his stomach, and pats his protruding belly proudly. "God bless America," he says with each pat. "Only here can someone become the Buddha."

I go to the back of the store and pull out the fold-up table and chairs the three of us always sit at. I have a small deli counter in the front, now empty, behind which used to lie wasted slabs of roast beef, ham, and turkey cut to look like the upper half of a cow's thigh, just before it becomes the ass. I spent two thousand dollars of borrowed money on it with the idea that perhaps my store could become a deli, and in becoming a deli, a restaurant, and in becoming a restaurant, a place that I could sit back and look proudly upon. I place the chairs right in front of the empty deli counter. I sit with my back against the glass. It's May 2. Since January, I've had exactly three deli orders (turkey, no mayo, wheat bread; turkey, mustard, wheat bread; turkey, just one slice), not a single one after lunchtime. Despite my recent efforts, there is nothing special to my store. It's narrow, shabby, and brightly lit, with a ceiling of fluorescent bulbs that hum for over an hour every morning after being turned on. I sell twenty-five-cent bags of potato chips, two-liter bottles of Pepsi, boxes of macaroni and cheese, diapers, soap, detergent, condensed milk in narrow aisles haphazardly arranged.

"Jo-Jo here yet?" Kenneth asks. Some days it's Joe from the Congo, or Joe-Joe Congo, or Congo Joe.

"Not yet."

"Africans. Congolese. You can never trust us to be on time."

"You are."

"I'm an engineer. I have to be precise. Precision is the name of my game. You say to be somewhere at eight-thirty, I'm there at eight-thirty. Not a minute later."

He pulls out a bottle of Johnnie Walker Black from his bag and places it on the table.

"How was today?" he asks me.

"Three hundred seventy-three dollars and eighty-four cents."

Kenneth shakes his head mournfully at the number. Almost nobody comes into the store anymore. It's been this way for months now, with each month a little worse than the one before. Business is slow, money is tight, and ever since Judith moved out of the neighborhood, I've been opening and closing my store at odd hours, driving away what few regular customers I still have left. Recently Kenneth tried to bring the subject up while we were alone in the store. He was looking at my accounts for April and shaking his head in dismay while tsking loudly to himself. There were ten days last month that were marked with a red zero, days that I hadn't even bothered to open the store, or that I had closed before any customers had a chance to come in.

"Why are you doing this?" he finally asked me. He held open the book so I could see exactly what he was talking about. "Do you even care?"

I shook my head, not knowing how to explain to him that there were no one-word responses or common phrases that I could turn to for an answer.

On a good day I have forty or maybe fifty customers. Most of them are stay-at-home moms or dads who've moved into one of the newly refurbished houses surrounding Logan Circle. They stop in during an afternoon stroll with their children dangling around their necks like amulets to ward off age, sickness, unemployment, rain, death. They buy bottled water, toothpaste, cleaning supplies, and, if their kids are old enough, one of the small five-cent pieces of candy I've learned to keep next to the register for just this purpose. On those good days, which come once or twice a week, I make just over four hundred dollars. I walk home at the end of the night feeling better, not only about my store, but about this country. I think to myself, America is beautiful after all. There is more here. Gas is cheap. This is not a bad place. Things could be worse. And what else could I have done?

"So then, you hate America today?" Kenneth says. He smiles a half-smile. He pours a little scotch into a Styrofoam cup he stole from his office and hands it to me. I know that if I let him, he would pull from his pocket the missing $26.16 and slide it into the cash register. Anything to make me feel better.

"With all my heart," I say to him.

Joseph's already drunk when he comes into the store. He strolls through the open door with his arms open. You get the sense when watching him that even the grandest gestures he may make aren't grand enough for him. He's constantly trying to outdo himself, to reach new levels of Josephness that will ensure that anyone who has ever met him will carry some lingering trace of Joseph Kahangi long after he has left. He's now a waiter at an expensive downtown restaurant, and after he cleans each table he downs whatever alcohol is still left in the glasses before bringing them back to the kitchen. I can tell by his slight swagger that the early dinnertime crowd was better than usual today.

Joseph is short and stout like a tree stump. He has a large

round face that looks like a moon pie. Kenneth used to tell him he looked Ghanaian.

"You have a typical Ghanaian face, Joe. Round eyes. Round face. Round nose. You're Ghanaian through and through. Admit it, and let us move on."

Joseph would stand up then and theatrically slam his fist onto the table, or into his palm, or against the wall. "I am from Zaire," he would yell out. "And you are a ass." Or, more recently, and in a much more subdued tone: "I am from the Democratic Republic of the Congo. Next week, it may be something different. I admit that. Perhaps tomorrow I'll be from the Liberated Land of Laurent Kabila. But today, as far as I know, I am from the Democratic Republic of the Congo."

Joseph kisses me once on each cheek after he takes his coat off.

"That's my favorite thing about you Ethiopians," he says. "You kiss each other on the cheeks all the time. It takes you hours to say hello and good-bye because you're constantly kissing each other. Kiss. Kiss. Kiss."

Kenneth pours Joseph a scotch and the three of us raise our cups for a toast.

"How is America today, Stephanos?" Joseph asks me.

"He hates it," Kenneth says.

"That's because he doesn't understand it." Joseph leans closer toward me, his large moon-pie face eclipsing my view of everything except his eyes, which are small and bloodshot, and look as if they were added onto his face as an afterthought.

"I've told you," he says. "This country is like a little bastard child. You can't be angry when it doesn't give you what you want."

He leans back deliberately in his chair and crosses his legs, holding the pose for two seconds before leaning over and resting both arms on his thighs.

"But you have to praise it when it comes close, otherwise it'll turn around and bite you in the ass."

The two of them laugh and then quickly pour back their drinks and refill their glasses. There is a brief silence as each struggles to catch his breath. Before either of them can tell me something else about America ("This country cares only about one thing . . ." "There are three things you need to know about Americans . . ."), I call out, "Bukassa." The name catches them off guard. They both turn and stare at me. They swirl their cups around and around to make sure it looks like they're thinking. Kenneth walks over to the map of Africa I keep taped on the wall right next to the door. It's at least twenty years old, maybe older. The borders and names have changed since it was made, but maps, like pictures and journals, have a built-in nostalgic quality that can never render them completely obsolete. The countries are all color-coded, and Africa's hanging dour head looks like a woman's head wrapped in a shawl. Kenneth rubs his hand silently over the continent, working his way west to east and then south until his index finger tickles the tip of South Africa. When he's finished tracing his hand over the map, he turns around and points at me.

"Gabon." He says it as if it were a crime I was guilty of.

"What about it?" I tell him, "I hear it's a fine country. Good people. Never been there myself, though."

He turns back to the map and whispers, "Fuck you."

"Come on. I thought you were an engineer," Joseph taunts him. "Whatever happened to precision?" He stands up and puts his large fat arm over Kenneth's narrow shoulders. With his other hand he draws a circle around the center of Africa. He finds his spot and taps it twice.

"Central African Republic," he says. "When was it?"

He scratches his chin thoughtfully, like the intellectual he always thought he was going to become, and has never stopped wanting to be.

"Nineteen sixty-four? No. Nineteen sixty-five."

"Nineteen sixty-six," I tell him.

"Close."

"But not close enough."

So far we've named more than thirty different coups in Africa. It's become a game with us. Name a dictator and then guess the year and country. We've been playing the game for over a year now. We've expanded our playing field to include failed coups, rebellions, minor insurrections, guerrilla leaders, and the acronyms of as many rebel groups as we can find—the SPLA, TPLF, LRA, UNITA—anyone who has picked up a gun in the name of revolution. No matter how many we name, there are always more, the names, dates, and years multiplying as fast as we can memorize them so that at times we wonder, half-jokingly, if perhaps we ourselves aren't somewhat responsible.

"When we stop having coups, we can stop playing," Joseph said once. It was the third or fourth time we had played, and we were guessing how long we could keep it up.

"I should have known that," Kenneth says. "Bukassa has always been one of my favorites."

We all have favorites. Bukassa. Amin. Mobutu. We love the ones known for their absurd declarations and comical performances, the dictators who marry forty women and have twice as many children, who sit on golden thrones shaped like eagles, declare themselves minor gods, and are surrounded by rumors of incest, cannibalism, sorcery, and magic.

"He was an emperor," Joseph says. "Just like your Haile Selassie, Stephanos."

"He didn't last as long, though," I remind him.

"That's because no one gave him a chance. Poor Bukassa. Emperor Bukassa. Minister of Defense, Education, Sports, Health, War, Housing, Land, Wildlife, Foreign Affairs, His Royal Majesty, King of the Sovereign World, and Not Quite But Almost the Lion of Judah Bukassa."

"He was a cannibal, wasn't he?" Kenneth asks Joseph.

"According to the French, yes. But who can believe the French? Just look at Sierra Leone, Senegal. Liars, all of them."

"The French or the Africans?"

"What difference does it make?"

We spend the next two hours alternating between shots and slowly sipped glasses of Kenneth's scotch. Inevitably, predictably, our conversations find their way home.

"Our memories," Joseph says, "are like a river cut off from the ocean. With time they will slowly dry out in the sun, and so we drink and drink and drink and we can never have our fill."

"Why do you always talk like that?" Kenneth demands.

"Because it is true. And that is the only way to describe it. If you have something different to say, then say it."

Kenneth leans his chair back against the wall. He's drunk and on the verge of falling.

"I will say it," he says.

He pours the last few drops of scotch into his cup and sticks his tongue out to catch them.

"I can't remember where the scar on my father's face is. Sometimes I think it is here, on the left side of his face, just underneath his eye. But then I say to myself, that's only because you were facing him, and so really, it was on the right side. But then

I say no, that can't be. Because when I was a boy I sat on his shoulders and he would let me rub my hand over it. And so I sit on top of a table and place my legs around a chair and lean over and I try to find where it would have been. Here. Or there. Here. Or there."

As he speaks his hand skips from one side of his face to the other.

"He used to say, when I die you'll know how to tell it's me by this scar. That made no sense but when I was a boy I didn't know that. I thought I needed that scar to know it was him. And now, if I saw him, I couldn't tell him apart from any other old man."

"Your father is already dead," I tell him.

"And so is yours, Stephanos. Don't you worry you'll forget him someday?"

"No. I don't. I still see him everywhere I go."

"All of our fathers are dead," Joseph adds.

"Exactly," Kenneth says.

It's the closest we've ever come to a resolution.

It's a few minutes past midnight when Joseph and Kenneth stand to go home. They both live in the suburbs, right outside of the city, in nearly identical, fully carpeted apartments with hardly any furniture besides the oversize televisions that they leave on even when they're not home. They both hate the city now.

Joseph kisses me once on each cheek before leaving. Kenneth slaps me on the back and says one more time, for good measure, "Keep fighting the good fight, Stephanos."

They pull away in Kenneth's badly worn used red Saab. Buying that car was Kenneth's first entry into a long-awaited form of American commerce that I think he imagined would lift him above the fray. Three years ago I went with him to a used-car dealership on the outskirts of a distant Virginia suburb to buy that car. He picked me up early on a Saturday morning when business was already slow and a few lost hours in the store didn't amount to much. He had rented a car for the occasion, a midsize sedan that placed him squarely in the middle class, of which he had just recently become a member. He wore a suit for the occasion, one cheaper than the ones he wears these days, but a suit nonetheless. He pulled the car up to my house and waited for me downstairs while leaning coolly against the passenger-side window, legs crossed. I wish for his sake there had been more people out there to see him because he looked wonderful. It wasn't just the clothes and the rented car, but an unadorned confidence that I had never seen him with before.

"How do I look, Stephanos?" he asked me as I walked out the front door. "Good, no?"

He had a habit back then, only recently abandoned, of ending his sentences with a question. He lifted his arms just high enough to reveal that the cuffs on his jacket were almost half an inch too short.

"Top class," I told him.

"You mean that, no? I really look good?"

"Of course you do."

Our drive to the dealership was a slow one. He eased his way prematurely into fading green lights, and took a slow, extended route around the neighborhood to reach the expressway. I didn't mind any of it. We had all suffered enough mockery and humiliation to last us well beyond our lifetimes, and if my role now was to serve as a blind, unflaggingly devoted cheerleader through whatever challenges and victories lay ahead, then I was all the happier for it.

We pulled into the dealership cautiously, as if every minor gesture of ours were being judged. We got out of the car, and rather than walk around the lot or enter the main office, Kenneth grabbed me by the wrist and said, "Wait, Stephanos. Let them come to us."

He resumed the pose he had taken in front of my house, except now, with the sun a little higher, he put on a pair of sunglasses to complete the portrait. As we stood outside and waited against the hood of the car, middle-aged American men in white short-sleeve shirts came in and out of the main office, walked leisurely through the aisles of cars, dabbed their brows with handkerchiefs that they then refolded back into their pockets, and never once passed anything more than a brief, one-eyed glance in our direction. We waited ten and then twenty minutes before we finally realized that no one was coming to us, regardless of what we wore or how long we stood there.

"Come on, Stephanos. Let's go," Kenneth finally said. "They don't have what I want."

Kenneth showed up at the store three days later in the red Saab. He came near the end of the day and dropped the keys on the register as if he had just plucked them from one of the aisles.

"Look at the label," he said.

There was a red-and-blue Saab key chain, and the heads of the two keys were each wrapped in rubber and stamped with the company logo.

"A Saab?" I asked him.

"Not bad, no?"

"Where is it?"

"Right out front. Go see for yourself."

Kenneth stayed in the store while I went to inspect his car. There were webs of rust along the rear tires, a dented front fender, and patches of faded paint along the passenger-side door. When I went back into the store I gave him a high-five. I lied and told him that the car was beautiful.

"Really? Beautiful?" he asked me.

"Beautiful," I told him.

I watch the car through the windows as Kenneth and Joseph miss their turn off the circle and have to drive around it again. The second time, they honk just for me as they pass by.

ב

When Judith bought the house next door to mine early last September it was an event that had once seemed so impossible that when I mentioned it to Joseph and Kenneth one night, it sounded more like a knock-knock joke than any plausible version of reality we had ever imagined. We were sitting at our table in the store, the doors and windows open so that we could hear the chatter of the kids in the street as we played cards and drank beer wrapped in brown paper bags, in homage to the men doing the same on the corner.

"Guess what?" I asked them.

"What?"

"Some white people just moved in."

"Where?"

"Next door."

"Next door to who?"

"Me."

"He's lying."

"I'm serious."

"Next door to *you*."

"Yes."

"In that house."

"I think they're going to fix it up."

"Why would white people want to live next to you?"

"I don't think they know I live here."

"How do you know?"

"I saw them."

"And what did they look like?"

"Tall. White."

"How many?"

"I only saw one."

"Well then, that proves nothing."

"She was searching in her purse for keys."

The house Judith was moving into was a beautiful, tragic wreck of a building and had been for years. A four-story brick mansion, it could have played the role of haunted house in any one of a hundred movies or books. Its elaborately tiled roof, flaking like dried skin, was echoed in the shutters that still clung out of stubbornness to the delicately molded windows arched like a pair of cartoon eyes on both sides of the house. The brick was almost obnoxious in its bright shade of red, redeemed at the last minute by the house's stature as the only one with color left on Logan Circle. There was a sad patch of grass in the front, and a rusted metal fence with a gate just barely hanging on to its hinges. The house had been abandoned for more than a decade, occupied briefly over the years by homeless men, crack addicts, and a small band of anarchists from Portland.

There were at least two dozen other houses like Judith's and mine surrounding Logan Circle. Four- and five-story mansions that had once belonged to someone of great import—a president's cousin, or aunt, or maybe nephew—but that over the years had been neglected, burned out, or in my case, divided into cheap, sometimes cockroach-infested, apartments. The houses cast long shadows over the circle and street, their rooftop shadows converging on the statue of General Logan, perched high on his horse in the center of the circle. When I moved into the neighborhood I did so because it was all I could afford, and because secretly I loved the circle for what it had become: proof that wealth and power were not immutable, and America was not always so great after all. The neighborhood, and by extension the city, had fallen, and every night I could see and hear that out of my living-room window.

Within a week of Judith's arrival an army of men descended on the house in squadlike formations. There were the plumbers, the electricians, the heating guys, the painters, the roofers, and the architect, who always came dressed in a well-tailored suit and stood leaning against the side of his silver Mercedes with a yellow hard hat on. Almost all of the men who worked on the house came into my store during their lunch breaks to buy a few dollars' worth of junk food. They were as reliable as the Jehovah's Witnesses who still made their weekly rounds across the neighborhood. And while I knew the workers would come and go, I took their presence at the time as a sign that things were improving, that the neighborhood was getting better and life was on the verge of changing. It was partly because of them and what they did to the house and others in the neighborhood that

I added the deli counter to my store in January, hoping that perhaps I, too, could profit from the houses that gleamed with their newly restored glory.

It was from the construction workers that I first found out some of the details of Judith's life—details that could, of course, come only from people who know your home so intimately they inevitably believe they've come to know something of you as well. Through them I learned that the woman was a lesbian bitch with too much money on her hands. She was fucking the architect on the side (you could tell by the way they always went off to some room when she came by), which explained why he was such a bastard himself and why he probably got the job. She wanted a bathroom on every floor of the house, which made no goddamn sense because why the fuck would she need four bathrooms when only two people would be living there? Her library was an entire floor and she wanted the whole thing with built-in bookcases and sliding doors to cover them. What kind of fucking person needed doors to cover their books? And her bedroom? It was half of the third floor. A whole fucking family could live in a room that size. There was no husband, boyfriend, or girlfriend, but she was a lesbian, you could bet on that. All you had to do was look at that short hair and nearly flat chest to see it.

It wasn't until the end of that September that I finally met the woman I had described to Joseph and Kenneth as tall and white. Until then I had seen her only once, in passing, out my bedroom window as she stood on the steps of the house and stared up at the roof. At first I had assumed that she was an agent of some city bureaucracy, assigned to the neighborhood to report on the condition of its aging buildings, to determine whether they were in need of repair or demolishment. Before Judith, these were the only reasons white people had ever come into the neighborhood: to deliver official notices, investigate crimes, and check up on the children of negligent parents. It wasn't until she began to rub her hand along the banister and chip away at the crumbling black paint that I realized her interest in the house was purely personal. She foraged through her purse, pulled out a set of keys, and nudged the door open with her shoulder: irrefutable signs of ownership.

Judith was sitting on the bottom steps of the house on an early fall afternoon with a little girl leaning back in between her legs when I came out of my house. I was dressed for a wedding, and as I turned to lock the door behind me, I heard her say, "What a beautiful garment." Her use of the word "garment" struck me most—it was polite, almost formal, as if the word had been inserted into her sentence at the last possible moment out of an instinctive sense of cultural diplomacy. I was dressed entirely in white. I had on white pants, with a white shirt that had a crucifix embroidered down the middle, over which I wore a finely woven shroud of white cotton. It was an outfit that meant nothing here, stripped as it was of all context. On the rare occasions that I still wore it, I did so expecting the taunts and stares of my neighbors and their children.

"Thank you," I said.

"What's it made of?"

"Cotton."

"Special occasion?"

"A wedding."

"Not your own, is it?"

"No. A cousin's."

She introduced herself by pointing to the house behind her and telling me she had just moved in. Her name, Judith—Judy—was the English counterpart to my cousin's name—Yodit. When I pointed that out she shook her head, bit down on her lower lip, and said, "No, no. That's much prettier than Judith. Much prettier." She was tall and narrow, with skinny arms and short brown hair cut just above her shoulders. She had a slightly crooked mouth and full lips that marked her face in a peculiar way. They made her mouth seem too large for her face, and her face too small for her head, so that there was something almost doll-like about her.

"You're right," I said. "It is."

We both pretended to laugh, after which she introduced me to her daughter, Naomi, a small, pretty girl with a skin tone closer to mine than her mother's.

"She's beautiful," I told her.

"Yes. You're right. She is," she said. She rubbed her hands over her daughter's head and then whispered something into her ear. The girl leaned her head back, looked up at her mother, and smiled. I could see the resemblance then. It was in the narrow angle of their faces, both of which sloped down into a smooth, pointed chin. When the girl turned back around and faced me I felt a hint of embarrassment and shame come over me. I knew I was being judged by this child as she refused to avert her gaze from mine.

The cab I had called to take me to the wedding pulled up then. It was an expense that I couldn't afford, but one that had nonetheless been demanded of me by the occasion. Judith and I said good-bye, it was nice to meet you, and then I was off to my cousin's wedding—a woman ten years younger than me, and of no real relationship to me beyond an affinity that our fathers had shared for each other in Ethiopia. After the wedding the photographs were taken at the National Botanical Gardens, most inside the greenhouse, in the shadow of yellow, purple, and red flora so large as to seem comical. There my cousin and her new husband met another newlywed Ethiopian couple also posing for pictures. They took three together, the two brides and two grooms standing on opposite sides of a blooming purple bush. And later that evening, during the reception, we heard that the same groom who had been standing on the opposite side of that bush only two hours earlier had died in the middle of his own reception.

Everyone grew somber when they heard the news whispered at their table. If there was one thing we all knew how to do, it was pay our respects to the dead. We all shook our heads, mumbled parts of the same prayers we had used for our fathers and friends, and then moved on, grateful in the way only other people's tragedies can make you.

Once construction on Judith's house had progressed far enough for her to move in near the end of October, I began to see her around the neighborhood more often. I often saw her reading on one of the benches across from General Logan on a late fall afternoon, undisturbed by the drunk men sleeping or stumbling around her. A whirlwind of fallen leaves and trash would occasionally rise around the base of Logan's statue and flit about in the air as if deliberately calling attention to itself. Judith, however, looked as indifferent to her surroundings as General Logan did on his horse, her legs properly crossed, one shoe dangling just slightly from her foot as she turned her head with the flip of each page. I admired her from a distance; the way she sat, confident and oblivious to the world, her hair sometimes caught in a gust of wind to reveal the long, elegant lines of her neck. She would sweep her hair back with one clean gesture that suggested unbroken concentration on whatever was in front of her.

She began to stop by the store on random afternoons to pick up a carton of milk or a piece of candy for her daughter, and we would chat briefly about the weather, the neighborhood, children.

"Do you have any?" she asked me once.

"None that I'll acknowledge. But I'm working on it."

"Too bad. It's easier if you know them."

"I'll try and remember that next time."

We waved to each other from across the circle and extended our conversations with each other whenever our paths crossed coming in or out of our houses. I wasn't the only one in the neighborhood to notice her. Of all the white people who had moved into Logan Circle over the past six months, she was the most visible, and not just because she spent her afternoons reading in the circle, or because she occasionally shopped in my store. It was Naomi, with her lighter than black but darker than white skin, sitting next to her on a bench, or walking with her hand in hand, who made people notice.

Mrs. Davis, who lived alone one floor below me, was the first to say something. It was the beginning of November and Judith had fully settled into her new home and become a fixture around the neighborhood. Her routine was familiar to those of us who watched. She was prone to midafternoon runs and reading in her living room with the curtains pulled back. The house looked beautiful now, especially at night with the single porch bulb shining down on the steps, which had also been smoothed out and worked over.

"You know that woman living next door?"

Mrs. Davis was standing outside as she normally did, leaning against the front fence, surveying every person and car that passed before her with what she believed was a keen and watchful eye for all things suspicious. For twenty-three years she had lived in this neighborhood, thirteen of which were spent in this house, first alone, and then with her husband, who passed away eight years ago. Over the years I had watched her go to church two, sometimes three times a week just, I believe, so she could escape the deafening silence that came with living alone in old age. In the summer she made feeble, halfhearted attempts at planting flowers in the weed-ridden patch of soil in front of the house. A geranium or tulip would bloom, only to die of neglect. In the fall and spring she stood outside and watched the children walk home from school with their arms around each other, and in the winter you could sometimes spot her wrapped in a blanket sitting on the couch nearest the front windows simply staring out vacantly onto the empty sidewalk and street, as if something only she remembered had occurred there, and now was the hour designated for remembering it. She had a habit of spitting out bits of food trapped between her teeth as she spoke to you, and in desperate moments of restlessness she was known to sweep the sidewalks and street free of litter. Anyone who didn't know her well and saw her pushing a broom back and forth from the front of her house to the curb thought she was mad. Those of us who knew her realized she was not mad, only bored and looking for the attention of her neighbors.

When Mrs. Davis asked me about Judith, she already knew the answer. I had caught her on several occasions watching us talk from her living-room window. She couldn't help smiling her perfect, wide smile to remind me of that.

"Yes, Mrs. Davis. I know her."

"Why do you think a woman like that would wanna live here? Doesn't seem right, does it?"

She had a small face with tightly bundled features, her eyes and nose closely set together, as if they had failed to grow since she was a child. When she asked me questions she rapped her fingers against the fence, showing off her hands, which had aged even better than the rest of her.

"It's a free country, Mrs. Davis. People can live where they like."

"What do you know about free countries? You didn't even know what that was till you came here last week, and now you're telling me people can live where they like. This isn't like living in a hut, you know. People around here can't just put their houses on their backs and move on."

She tried not to laugh at her own joke, but failed, and her face disappeared once more under a row of shining, perfect white teeth.

"What can you do? The neighborhood's changing," I told her. I had said the same thing at least a dozen times before, when the first few houses in the neighborhood were sold, when a restaurant opened up a few blocks away, when up the street the discount grocery store with two rows dedicated solely to generic goods shut down. The neighborhood's changing, things are changing, it's not like it used to be, I can't believe how much it's changed, who would have thought it could change so quickly, nothing is permanent, everything changes; the passive and helpless observations of people stuck living on the sidelines.

The change wasn't gradual, or rapid, but somewhere in between. Two years ago I would spot the occasional odd face walking past my storefront windows—a white woman carrying groceries home early in the evening, a man jogging with his dog shortly after dusk—and think little of it. It wasn't until the summer before Judith moved into the neighborhood that the change began in earnest, which is to say it became inevitable. Moving vans began to arrive on some of the blocks on the first of every month—the long, full-length professional ones that came fully loaded with overweight men wearing shirts barely large enough to stretch over their swollen guts. I spent most of one Sunday afternoon in July watching them move furniture into a house just outside the circle, less than a hundred feet away from my store. They unloaded two gilded mirrors and an antique desk, along with a pair of sofas with pillows so large and comfortable that I imagined myself asking if I could sit, for just a few minutes. A handful of other people were watching with me from the other side of the street. The entire time we stood out there I heard only one person say anything at all, nothing more than a simple phrase, "white people."

"You spend all day in that store by yourself and that's all you got to say," Mrs. Davis said.

"Unfortunately, yes. Can I get you anything tomorrow?"

"Get me some milk. I don't want nothing that's expired, though. I may be old but that doesn't mean I want my milk to be."

"Of course not, Mrs. Davis."

She stepped to the side and let me pass through the gate, kissing me once on the cheek as I went by.

A few days later, Naomi came into the store by herself. It was the first time I had seen her without her mother. On the few occasions Judith had brought her to the store, Naomi had simply stood quietly next to the door, hands clasped behind her back as she surveyed the contents of the aisle in front of her. I had asked her once if she wanted to come inside and take a look around. Her response had been swift and definitive.

"I can see everything from here," she said. It was an honest answer that I couldn't argue with.

When Naomi came into the store on her own, she became what almost all children want to be: stubbornly independent. She pushed the door open with both hands, her feet running in place behind her until it gradually began to give. Once inside, she took a swipe at a piece of hair that had fallen in front of her eyes, and as she stood there in light gray slacks and a frilly button-down blue shirt, it was possible to see for a second at least one of the women I imagine she's going to become.

She walked through the store as if she knew where everything was already. Up one aisle and then down the other, until she had plodded her way through them all, without so much as glancing at any of the items on the shelves. When she came down the last aisle, she did so with her gaze firmly fixed on the floor, her feet clomping heavily with each step as if she were determined to crush the tile beneath her. She walked right past the counter and straight to the door, which she again struggled with in the same determined manner for a few seconds, and then she was gone. Had she not left a trail of muddy footprints down the aisle, I might not have believed she had ever been there, so quickly and resolutely did she pass through.

Minutes later, Judith came running into the store by herself, just as well dressed as her daughter, except for her hair, which lay tossed to the side in a stringy mess. She scanned the aisles quickly before turning and yelling to me, "Have you seen Naomi?"

I told her what had just happened, and before I finished she was off. I grabbed my keys, locked the door, and left. Before I took even a dozen steps outside, though, I heard Judith's voice yelling and crying at the same time: "Stop doing this! Never, ever do this again!"

She and Naomi were in the alley right around the corner. Judith was on her knees, shaking Naomi by the shoulders, while her daughter just stood there, visibly indifferent to what her mother was saying. I watched them silently from a few feet away. Tears had begun to stream down Judith's face as she shook and yelled at her daughter. When Judith finally gave in and embraced her, I turned around and went back to my store.

Later that afternoon, Judith came back and offered what I could tell had become a routine apology for her. She repeated the words as if she were reading them from a manual: "I'm sorry about what happened this afternoon. Naomi can be difficult. Thanks for all your help."

"That's okay," I told her. "I used to run away all the time when I was a child."

She smiled back gratefully at me. If there was one thing I understood about people, it was how far even the smallest gesture of sympathy could go when needed.

"And how did your mom get you to stop?"

"She didn't. That's how I ended up here."

She gave a slight, courteous laugh for the attempt.

"Normally she just hides in some corner of the house when she gets upset. But every once in a while she manages to escape before I can stop her."

"Have you thought of chains?"

"Illegal."

"How about a cage?"

"Still illegal."

"Sleeping pills?"

"Tylenol PM count?"

"Close enough."

"Then yes."

✤

Judith and Naomi became regulars at my store after that day. In a new house, in a new neighborhood, it became a safe, familiar place for the both of them for one reason only: Naomi had picked it as the place to be seen. The hideously green tiled floors and the bad fluorescent lighting, the five tightly packed aisles could, if seen often enough, or through the right eyes, have an air of warmth to them. Of at least that I was certain.

If it was early enough in the afternoon, Judith let Naomi come to the store alone. Our first few tries at conversation were awkward and painful. We missed each other completely.

"How do you like your new neighborhood?" I asked her.

"Why do you always ask me questions?" she asked me. She turned her back on me then and pretended to browse through the aisles of cheap processed foods, none of which she would ever need. After that she left and didn't come back for two days. But we persevered. We progressed in stages. The next time Naomi came to the store, she walked straight over to the map of Africa I kept taped on the wall.

"Do you know what that is?" I asked her.

She shook her head in contempt and didn't say a word. Of course she knew, and I was made a fool for asking. I showed her where Ethiopia was and put my finger on the star that marked the capital. I told her that was where I was from and where my mother and brother still lived.

"Do you have a picture of them?" she asked me.

"Only one old one."

"That's not good," she said. "You should have more. Don't you miss them?"

"Yes, I do," I told her. "But I try not to."

She stared at me with her wide eyes and blinked twice.

Naomi began coming to the store more often after that day. By the middle of November she was coming at least three times a week, more often five or six. She came straight from school or early on a Saturday morning. Some afternoons she simply stood next to the register and rocked back and forth on her heels while chewing a piece of gum. On other days she read pink paperback novels whose plots she summarized for me in a hundred words or less. I gave her little packages of candy to save for later, and I could tell by the way she quickly tucked them into her pockets without ever reading the label that was precisely what she did. In exchange for the candy, Naomi reported to me the whole wide world as it came to her every day.

"I saw this kid getting beat up in the alley yesterday."

"Two guys were kissing each other on the mouth near the park."

"There was this boy down the block peeing in front of some-one's house."

"The old woman that lives next door to us was sweeping the street this morning."

Kids pushed and beat one another up on almost every block; they flashed gang signs, shouted insults, and made threats. Nothing, however, seemed to alarm Naomi, and when she told me what she had seen, she did so without fear or hesitation, as if she already knew that the only way to live was to take all of the things you saw at face value.

When I asked her questions, she always just shrugged her shoulders and came up with a one-word answer.

"How was school today?"

"Fine."

"How's your mom?"

"Fine."

"What's fine about her?"

"Everything."

"What did you learn today?"

"Nothing."

"You mean the entire day, your teacher taught you nothing new? Not a single fact, or word?"

"Nope."

"You think you're pretty funny, don't you?"

"Yup."

With each "nope" or "yup" she made sure to drag out the vowel so she could pop her lips hard on that final consonant.

We read the newspaper together, which was her way of showing me how smart she was. Naomi was eleven years old, and she took pride in being able to shake her head at the world. She was convinced that American foreign policy in the Middle East was a failure, that a two-state solution in Israel was inevitable, and that enough wasn't being done about the global AIDS crisis. She tucked and folded the creases in the *Washington Post* with an agility fitting an old man, and even the way she leaned against the counter, her head resting on her chin as she thumbed her way through the articles, spoke of a wisdom that seemed to belong more to her mother than to her.

"You know, kids shouldn't talk like that," I told her once.

She shrugged her shoulders again, letting her eyes drop to the floor in a way that seemed rehearsed.

"I know," she said. "But I'm not a kid."

"What are you, then?"

"I'm an adult."

"You're eleven."

"And how old are you?"

"A lot older."

"So what's your point? I'm supposed to be stupid until I'm a lot older?"

"Exactly. Why do you think people like kids so much?"

One afternoon we ran out of things to talk about, so we invented some. By the end of Naomi's time in the store that day, we had created an entire alternate universe populated exclusively with animals. The world was made simply enough. Standing in front of the register, her elbows just barely perched on the counter, Naomi had done what she did best. She commanded.

"Tell me a story," she said.

I remember looking at her and wondering where that instinct to dictate came from. She was too young for almost everything she said and did, and yet when given the chance, she seized every moment of childishness that I could offer her. Judith had struck me as deliberate and patient in every one of her actions, while Naomi acted only on desire, indifferent to consequences and pitfalls, free of restraint.

She slumped her head down into her folded arms and gazed at me with those wide, comic eyes of hers, and for the first time since meeting her I wished that she were mine entirely.

"What kind of story?" I asked her.

She shrugged her shoulders.

"Something funny?"

She nodded.

"What else?" I asked her.

"There should be animals," she said.

"What kind?"

"You pick."

"A monkey?" I asked her.

"Two monkeys," she said.

"Okay. Two monkeys. What do they do?"

"They own a store."

"What kind of store?"

"A big one."

And so, from the beginning, even the animals were a few steps ahead of me. The two monkeys, whom we never had to name, had the largest grocery store for miles. They had a house on the lake, stocks, cars, and more friends than they knew what to do with. They threw lavish parties and were the toast of the jungle. Most important, they had Henry the chauffeur. He bled into our lives immediately. Some afternoons, he was all we talked about.

"Henry's taking me to the movies tonight," Naomi would say.

"He was just here," I would tell her.

"Was he looking for me?"

"Of course. I think he was even a bit sad when he left."

Henry drove us to concerts and plays, and on occasion to the summer homes we created for ourselves along the coast. Once he forgot to pick Naomi up from school, which was why, she explained, she hadn't been able to see me that day.

"Henry," she said, "messed up big time."

Henry was responsible for the broken radiator in my store one afternoon. He was responsible for the dwindling supply of candy one week. On better days he gave us advice on our taxes, suggested investments, brokered deals, and when life turned unexpectedly, bore the brunt of our failures and mistakes, our disappointments, accidents, mishaps, frustrations, and angers.

ф

The only rule Judith had for Naomi was that she always had to be home before five, just as the early winter sun was beginning to set. Judith picked that hour because it had been at roughly that time of day that a young man had approached her on her way home from my store and asked her if she liked to suck black dick. As she was walking past General Logan, the young man pulled out his penis and then broke out in laughter and went running back to his friends, who were watching from the benches only a few feet away.

"It wasn't scary," Judith said. "Just humiliating. Which is maybe even worse."

If Naomi wasn't home by four-thirty, Judith came to the store to pick her up. How long Naomi stayed was always a matter of her own choice. On the afternoons I was busy she left almost as soon as she arrived. "You're boring," she would tell me, and she would leave angry, or she would stay until the last possible moment, eager to do anything except return to her mother. Judith not only tolerated her daughter's fierceness, she loved her all the more for it.

"You know, I keep wondering what I would have done if Naomi had been there when that kid came up to me. I keep thinking that she would have handled it better than I did."

How Judith handled it was by turning around and walking slowly past her house until she found a bus stop, where she sat and cried for just a minute.

"I told myself that if I looked determined enough, he couldn't touch me. My hands were shaking so hard I had to clasp them in front of me while I walked. I could hear him laughing with his friends for about a block, and then they just stopped and moved on."

We had all of our conversations in front of Naomi, with Judith on one side of the counter and me on the other, Naomi sitting on a stool somewhere in between the two of us. She was looking through the real-estate ads in the back of the *Washing-*

ton Post's Sunday magazine while Judith told me about the incident.

"I would have kicked him where it counts," Naomi said, her eyes still supposedly focused on the ads.

"I don't doubt for a second that you would have, honey."

"Why did he say that to you?"

"I don't know. I think he thought it was all just a joke."

Judith leaned over and caressed her daughter's hair. "We should go. It's getting late," she said.

"You want me to walk you home?"

"No. We're fine. Plus, I got my little kickboxer with me."

Naomi let her mother pick her up off her stool, and she even let her hold her for almost a minute before she wriggled herself free. It was six-thirty on a Friday night—late and dark enough to have brought out a few of the kids who would settle onto the corner for the rest of the evening. The two of them walked out of my store hand in hand, past a few snickers and "Pssssts" and "Heys" as if they were oblivious to everything besides each other.

3

Kenneth calls me at home early the next morning just as I'm about to leave my apartment.

"Why aren't you at the store yet?" he asks me. It's the first thing he says, and the only reason he called to begin with. He's been calling me at least once a week since April. He calls me at home early in the morning, or at the store in the middle of the day to see if I'm performing my shopkeeper duties, first and foremost of which is to be open. Now that it's May, he seems determined to let me know that I can expect more of the same from him. In the background I can hear other phones ringing and a low rumble of indistinguishable voices. I've never been to Kenneth's office, but I imagine a busy row of men in identical suits picking and hanging up their phones in unison.

"I was on my way there," I tell him.

"It's almost nine," he says. I look at the clock hanging on the wall across from me. I hadn't considered the time yet. There are already too many hours in the day; to worry about any one in particular is pointless.

"I know what time it is."

"Joseph and I were planning on coming back to the store tonight," he tells me.

"You don't have to."

"I know."

He hangs up abruptly then. This is what he believes men in power can do. They can dismiss with a wave of the hand and never think twice about it. There are those who wake each morning ready to conquer the day, and then there are those of us who wake only because we have to. We live in the shadows of every neighborhood. We own corner stores, live in run-down apartments that get too little light, and walk the same streets day after day. We spend our afternoons gazing lazily out of windows. Somnambulists, all of us. Someone else said it better: we wake to sleep and sleep to wake.

I leave for the store half an hour later, hoping, however foolishly, to catch what's left of the morning rush-hour crowd. The sidewalks and street are practically deserted; everyone but me and a few morning joggers has already reached their destination. The emptiness is nice, though. As I walk through the circle I decide to stop and take a seat on one of the new benches across from General Logan to listen to the birds chattering away loudly in the trees. There's an arc of benches on either side of the statue. The benches have new black lacquer paint, and behind the benches are thick layers of startlingly fresh green sod where only dust and scattered clumps of crabgrass and weeds used to grow. When I opened my store ten years ago, Logan Circle was still predominately poor, black, cheap, and sunk in a depression that had struck the city twenty years earlier and never left. Most of the streetlights that surrounded the circle were burned out, leaving the neighborhood perpetually pitched into a strange half-darkness more frightening than pure black. Before the newly formed General Logan Circle Statue Association restored the statue last month it was chipped, defaced, and smeared with human, dog, and bird shit. Drunk old men, their foreheads wrinkled, their pants barely buckled around their waists, rambled around the statue's benches in the afternoon and evening muttering to themselves and one another. The benches smelled of urine, and even the pigeons that strolled around the grass in search of thrown-away chicken bones and bread had a sad, desolate look to them, as if they knew by instinct that this was where their breed belonged. The old men have mostly shuffled on. A few, on occasion, still stumble around the circle, and even though I've never looked at any of their faces up close, I imagine there's something approaching shock and wonder as they look up at General Logan, whose bronze exterior is now clear enough for me to see my reflection in, and who looks down on all of us with the glimmering sheen of a privately funded cleaning job. I think if he were alive now he would have to say this is progress; that a society that fails to properly remember its dead and fallen heroes is a society not worth remembering at all.

The birds cackle away in their treetops, and after watching them hop idly from branch to branch for another half hour, I finally decide it's time for me to rise and join the forces of the working world. I take my time cutting through the circle. It's a few minutes after ten by the time I finally reach my store and lift open the metal grate that covers the front door. There's a morning ritual that comes with opening a store. I lift the metal grates, and then tug down the white plastic blinds that block out all light until they spring back up. I turn on the lights and wait for their mechanical hum to fill the room. I make a general assessment. Shelves, windows, cash register are all in place. The ceiling remains, the tiles on the floor have held. Everything is precisely as it should be. Even now, after all these years, this continues to amaze me. It seems as if time stands completely still at the close of each day, and is resumed only by my return. Sometimes I like to think that if I waited ten or twenty years before opening my store, I could return to find it completely unchanged.

Today I swing the front door wide open and let the wind make a mess of the papers still sitting on the counter. It's May 3, and purchase orders still unfulfilled from the previous month are piled a few inches high, along with a stack of receipts and bills that I can't afford to pay. It will rain today. You can smell it in the air, a midmorning spring shower that will last at least into the afternoon.

I gather the dust from the four corners of the store and usher it out the door. It erupts into a brief plume that's dissolved by the wind as soon as it hits the open air. The morning is quiet. The rain comes and fills the gutters and makes a puddle out of the patch of grass next to my store. Women trickle in, armed with their first-of-the-month government subsidy checks. They shop in small quantities: a few individual rolls of toilet paper; small bags of diapers; and can after can of processed soup. Until recently, most of my customers were teenagers on their way home from school, and on Friday and Saturday nights, single men browsing through the aisles of prostitutes who surrounded the circle after dark. The teenagers bought the chips and candy; the men bought the condoms behind the counter. More often than not, both opened them right after leaving the store, leaving a trail of candy wrappers and condom boxes on the sidewalk out front. A social worker who used to come through the neighborhood on the weekends told me the men did that to save time, and that if I ever stepped into the alley behind the store, I could see them putting the condoms on. She always bought a dozen candy bars for the women when she came in. They needed it, she said, to keep up their blood-sugar level.

Most of the women who worked on the circle also came to my store at one point or another. Those who came regularly flirted and shoplifted a bag of chips or a can of soda, knowing all along that I could see them but didn't care. They had names like Chocolate and Velvet, always things that you could touch or taste because the imagination is nothing if not tactile. On summer nights, traffic backed up for blocks leading into and out of the circle as a uniquely democratic blend of cars—Mercedes, Volvos, rusted Plymouths, and boxcar Chevys—lined up to choose from the women who ringed the circle in their bright neon outfits like a cheap, tawdry crown. If I stayed open late on the weekends back then, I could make as much in one night as I do in one week now. The men buying the diapers, ice cream, and tampons they had supposedly left home for, and the women, newly minted but still with only enough money to buy another can of soda to keep them awake, all came together for just enough hours every week to make me a living that I no longer judged as honest or decent, but accepted as a matter of standard fact somewhere in between yes, we all must die, and the sun is ninety-three million miles away.

There are hardly any women left on the circle now. They have vanished not into thin air, but into a different space or reality, as if they had all collectively taken flight and migrated to another climate. Around the circle, the question is still asked, although not as frequently: what happened to all the hos?

In the afternoon a short line of kids on their way home from school jostles to get in. The children fill the store with their out-size presence, shouting and screaming at one another because everything to them is urgent and desperate. One of them, a bald-headed boy with wide, emphatic eyes that remind me of Naomi's when she wants something from me or her mother, picks up a candy bar and slides it into the sleeve of his puffy coat, where it disappears into the warm nook of his bent wrist. He looks up at me for a second to see if I've caught him. His eyes say it all. They say, "This is what I want. All you have to do is let me have it." I agree, and with a smile and a simple nod of my head, he walks off. He's happy, and for a few seconds I'm happy for him.

Just as quickly as the crowd of children appeared, it vanishes, disappearing into the neighborhood in discrete clumps of twos and threes, with a few children wandering alone in the rear, their trail suggestive of a hierarchy of social order that leaves some muttering songs and games to themselves and others basking in the glow of friends and admirers. I'm left alone; the rest of the afternoon is so quiet that I can finish reading the paperback novel I checked out from the library the day before. From the first day I opened the store, I've kept a book close at hand so that every hour of even the quietest days has been filled with at least one voice other than my own. My first, a present from Joseph, was a paperback copy of a V. S. Naipaul novel. On the inside he wrote in his usual overstated manner: *To a new beginning, Stephanos. The journey is not over yet.* It was a not-so-subtle reference to my similarity to Saleem, the store owner in the novel, but more important, one of the few openly hopeful and enthusiastic remarks ever to come from Joseph's lips or hand. For that reason alone I've kept the book prominently displayed behind the counter all these years, and while Joseph and I have never talked about the book, every now and then he'll enter the store with his arms open and declare, "Saleem, you're both still here."

"Of course we are," I always tell him. "Where else do we have to go?"

Over the years I've read roughly one book every two days, few of which I have ever owned. No one tells you this at the beginning, but the days of a shopkeeper are empty. There are hours of silence punctuated briefly with bursts of customers who come and go within the span of a few minutes. The silence becomes a cocoon in which you can hear only your voice echoing; the real world in which you live begins to fade into a past that you have tried to put to rest. I began to check books out from the library in groups of four in order to make sure I had more than enough to read for the week. I knew I had time, and on particularly slow days, I had more of it than I knew what to do with, a problem that posed a risk greater than I was willing to bear. I felt it especially in the early days of the store. Left alone behind the counter, I was hit with the sudden terrible and frightening realization that everything I had cared for and loved was either lost or living on without me seven thousand miles away, and that what I had here was not a life, but a poorly constructed substitution made up of one uncle, two friends, a grim store, and a cheap apartment.

When asked by my uncle Berhane why I had chosen to open a corner store in a poor black neighborhood when nothing in my life had prepared me for such a thing, I never said that it was because all I wanted out of life now was to read quietly, and alone, for as much of the day as possible. I left him and his modest two-bedroom apartment in the suburbs in order to move to Logan Circle, a decision he has yet to understand or forgive me for, despite what he says. He used to have the grandest ambitions for me when I first arrived from Ethiopia. "Just wait and see," he would tell me in that soft-spoken, eloquent voice of his. "You will be an engineer or a doctor. I only wish your father could have lived to see it." Tears would well up in his eyes sometimes as he spoke about the future, which he believed could only be filled with better and beautiful things. Here in Logan Circle, though, I didn't have to be anything greater than what I already was. I was poor, black, and wore the anonymity that came with that as a shield against all of the early ambitions of the immigrant, which had long since abandoned me, assuming they had ever really been mine to begin with. As it was, I did not come to America to find a better life. I came here running and screaming with the ghosts of an old one firmly attached to my back. My goal since then has always been a simple one: to persist unnoticed through the days, to do no more harm.

In my monthly letters and phone calls to my mother and brother in Ethiopia, I tell them only that I own my own business, and that business is okay. Never good. Never bad. Simply okay. Could be better. Grateful it's not worse. I send them money once every few months when I can afford to, even though I know they don't need it. I do it because I am in America, and because sending money home is supposed to be the consolation prize for not being home. For Christmas last year my mother sent me a money order worth three hundred dollars more than all of the money I had ever sent. I still have the receipt in the nightstand next to my bed from when I cashed it.

✤

At six p.m. the temperature is still hovering near eighty, a definite sign of an impending hot and brutal summer. The few people who pass through at this time of day come in with their faces red and shiny with sweat. They stock up on bottled water before returning to their early-evening strolls and centrally air-conditioned homes. I make a mental note to myself: if possible, buy more water. I watch an old, beat-up Chevy drive around the circle three times, looking for something or someone that is no longer there. The sun makes the leftover rain on the roof sparkle as it winds around the block. There is a slow, lumbering quality to the day. I keep the air conditioner off and the door open.

Joseph and Kenneth come to the store together this time. They arrive almost an hour earlier than usual. Kenneth is still dressed in his suit and Joseph's wearing jeans with a University of Michigan sweatshirt that's far too heavy for the warm May night. Joseph kisses me once on the cheek. With the store still open, Kenneth has nothing to say, so he shakes my hand vigorously while trying out his new English accent.

"How you doing, ol' chap? Life treating you well these days?"

The two of them stand on opposite sides of the counter, leaning against the glass panes while flipping through the day's newspapers. By most accounts, it has been a decent day for the world. Inflation is low. Countries all across the globe are negotiating deals, hammering out truces, while their leaders shake hands on the cover of the *Washington Post* under headlines of restored hope and promises of cooperation. Even Africa has done well for itself today.

"Look," Kenneth calls out, holding open a copy of the newspaper so we can see the picture of Laurent Kabila that he's tapping proudly. "Laurent is coming through." He reads the brief article with an ironic enthusiasm. There are only a hundred and fifty words to the entire piece.

"You could learn something from him, Jo-Jo. That Kabila's a good man. A role model for all you Congolese."

"You said the same about Mobutu," Joseph says.

"That was just a joke. It was only because I liked his last name. Sese Seko. Sese Seko. I could say it over and over. But Kabila's a man of his word. He's the future of Africa's leaders."

"He will be dead within a year. Or he will never leave. It is always one or the other."

Kenneth leans his elbows back against the counter and stretches out his long lanky legs. "Help me out here, Stephanos."

"Dead within two years," I tell him.

At seven-thirty I close the doors to the store. Neither Joseph nor Kenneth asks me why I'm closing early, or whether it's been a good day, since no one has entered since they arrived. I don't add up the register because I've already done the math in my head. I know just how little I've earned. I pull a handful of bills out of the drawer and stuff them into my pocket, as if they were inconsequential.

Kenneth throws his arm around my shoulder and says, "Come on, Stephanos. It's time to leave." He squeezes my shoulder once, firmly, for encouragement.

Without asking or worrying about where we're going, I get into Kenneth's car with the two of them and we pull away from the store. We drive past my house, and what's left of Judith's, without pausing at the stop sign on the corner. The idea is to leave this neighborhood and store as quickly as possible, to rush headlong into the sun, which is just now setting. The entire flat skyline of the city is tinged with a pinkish hue that hardly seems real. We roll our windows down. In the backseat, Joseph puts his feet up and closes his eyes as the wind whips over his face. We all breathe in deeply. Kenneth cuts down one narrow side street after another to avoid traffic; the trees, flowers, and bushes are all in bloom. There is something unsettling about spring in D.C., a cautionary tale of overindulgence and inflated expectations that seems embedded in the grass and in the trees. I thought I had long since learned to keep those expectations in check, but it happens anyway, doesn't it? We forget who we are and where we came from, and in doing so, believe we are entitled to much more than we deserve.

In just a few minutes, we pull up in front of the Royal Castle, which from the outside still looks like the Chinese restaurant it had once been. The red awning and generic Asian typeface cast against a gold background stayed even after the menu had been reduced to buffalo wings, french fries, and hamburgers, and the large circular booths with the lazy Susans were replaced with stages, poles, and a row of chairs that remind me of a high school auditorium.

Instead of arguing or protesting, Joseph and I follow Kenneth in. We take a table in the back of the club, which is entirely empty except for us. Our isolation feels ridiculous. There's no one else to share our shame with, and when a topless waitress comes over to take our order, none of us can muster enough courage to look her in the face.

"Why are we here, Ken?"

"Because, Stephanos. This is what people do at the end of a hard day."

As if to prove his point, he undoes the top button on his shirt and loosens his tie a few inches. I've never met his boss, but I can hear his voice ringing in the back of Kenneth's head. "Still fighting the good fight, Kenneth?" it says.

We order three scotches, drink them quickly, and order three more. Women come and go off the stage every three and a half minutes, dancing halfheartedly to the '80s pop songs I used to love listening to in my store. Prince. INXS. The Cure. When they finish dancing they saunter over to our table and introduce themselves. They all have names from Greek and Roman mythology: Venus, Apollonia, Aphrodite—names that promise an unattainable bit of love and heaven. Before they can offer us anything, we hand them two singles each, and Kenneth tells them all that they're beautiful.

"Beautiful," he says, with his lips pursed, eyes turned to the ceiling in a feigned state of ecstatic reverie.

The drinks are ten dollars, and each one lasts for exactly three songs, which is equal to three dancers, which means we're spending about a dollar a minute, and that in sixty-eight minutes, I will have spent all the money I earned that day.

I take my last eight dollars out of my pocket and lay it on the table.

"Once that's done, so am I."

Joseph slides the bills back toward me. "Keep it," he says. "The rest of the evening is on me."

Kenneth pours back his scotch and slides the glass across the table so it almost falls on my lap. "No," he says. "The rest of the evening is on me."

They go back and forth for several minutes, each one insisting repeatedly that the "evening is on me" even though it's been clear from the start that Kenneth will be the one to pay. Still, what matters just as much as the outcome is how they get there. With the decision settled, Kenneth hands control over the rest of the night to Joseph, who places one hand on each of our backs and says, "Gentlemen, it is time for us to go."

There is nothing left of downtown D.C. by the time we walk outside. The city has emptied itself of its bureaucrats, politicians, lawyers, secretaries, diplomats, lobbyists, and bankers. The shutters are pulled down in front of all the storefronts, and graffiti has been scrawled all over them. *Beso. Crazy Nigga. East Capitol Crew.* The only people we pass on the street are all well dressed and well heeled, on their way home to the suburbs of Virginia or to one of the handful of luxurious restaurants that stand as clearly isolated from one another as a pair of trees in an open plain. The Capitol's white dome seems to hover in front of us, and if I turn just a little to the right, I can see the red eye sitting at the peak of the Washington Monument. There is no mystery left in any of those buildings for us, and at times I wonder how there ever could have been.

I stop in the middle of the road as we cross the street toward the car and look up and hard while Kenneth and Joseph walk on. I'm waiting to see if I can recall that emotion now—a silent, almost fearful awe that came when I first saw each building from a passing van, and that continued to come involuntarily for years afterward. My mother and father both claimed to have felt something similar every time they saw the emperor in Ethiopia— power embodied, as it were, in a single man.

I wink at the monument, salute the Capitol, and then run to catch up with Joseph and Kenneth, who are both already sitting in the car waiting for me.

"What were you doing back there, Stephanos?" Joseph asks me as I slide into the backseat.

I shrug. I don't know what to tell him, but he gives me a grin that says he already knows. After we finished our shifts at the Capitol Hotel, the three of us often spent the rest of our evenings perched on one of the benches across from the White House, or on the tree-lined paths leading up to the Lincoln Memorial.

"Look at those buildings," Joseph said once. "I would

have . . ." He stopped there, stuck in midsentence. It was one of the few times in all the years I have known him that he has ever been speechless. We rarely talked about the buildings explicitly, but I know that Joseph and Kenneth both spent hours standing in front of Lincoln's massive, imposing figure, seated on his throne with an indifferent gaze cast toward the city. During his first few months in America, Joseph had memorized the Gettysburg Address off the memorial's walls, and spent several nights watching the sun rise from its steps. It's been years since either of them has gone near those buildings, and how could you blame them? Reality has settled in, and they're both still waiting to recover.

We decide to end our evening at a small, dark, crowded bar on the northwest edge of the city. The crowd tonight is mixed. A half-dozen Nigerians, all friends with the owner, are pressed up against the bar, loudly ordering drinks and shots for one another. At the other end is an old white man with a beard drinking slowly by himself. Scattered throughout the booths and tables in the back are a couple dozen young white kids—the first to live in this neighborhood in thirty years. Kenneth and I slide into a booth and begin to drink. Joseph goes to the back of the bar and puts a dollar into the jukebox. We've been waiting for this moment to one degree or another since our first drink of the night. It takes about fifteen more minutes before the song begins, and with the first chord, we raise our glasses and toast. When the refrain starts, the three of us lean forward and sing along:

But you won't fool the children of the revolution.
No you won't fool the children of the revolution.

Over and over, until the song ends, by which point we've all finished our drinks and are ready for another.

The first time we heard that song we were sitting two booths farther back. We still worked at the Capitol Hotel; Joseph and Kenneth were sharing an apartment just a few blocks away from the bar. The song played, and Joseph stood up drunkenly and declared, "That is us. We are the children of the revolution." His accent was heavier then, weighted with tinges of French that struggled under a formal locution to come through. It took him several tries before we understood what he was saying, each attempt punctuated by an emphatic thrust toward the air holding the music, and in holding the music, holding Joseph as well. When we finally did understand him, Kenneth and I stood up, and together the three of us nodded our heads to the words we barely understood, the refrain repeating its unintended sympathies over and over.

Now, when the song is over, it's hard not to laugh at our misplaced enthusiasm. We had been in America for only a couple of years when we first heard it, and we did believe that we were children of a revolution, and not only because we were willing to be grand. We all had stories of families we missed and would never see again. We spoke in our broken English of Africa's tyrannies, which had yet to grow tedious. And we had our own stories of death and violence to match.

The song plays two more times over the course of the next two hours, and each time, like children being coaxed into a conversation, we sing along.

4

The first time Judith invited me over for dinner, she had Naomi slip a note into my mailbox.

Dear Mr. Stephanos,
   My mother and I would like to invite you to our house for dinner. On November 28. We would be very happy if you could come.

                                          Judith and Naomi

The letter arrived the day before Thanksgiving and carried me through the holiday. It was written in Naomi's delicate, tiny handwriting on a canary yellow piece of stationery that had Judith's name at the bottom. It was folded into a square small enough to fit into the center of my palm. Three days after getting the letter, I closed my store one hour early for the first time in years. It was an exceptionally cold night, and by seven-thirty an almost impenetrable hush had slipped over the neighborhood. Some people had rushed home from work, while others never left their house to begin with. The few people who came into the store that evening did so just to escape the cold. They lingered for ten or fifteen minutes over whatever it was they had supposedly come in to buy, and then left abruptly, feigning disappointment or frustration as they shook their heads, blew into their hands, and tucked their chins into their collars.

I went home early and changed into a neatly pressed button-down white shirt and a pair of slightly worn gray wool slacks Kenneth had handed down to me. The cuff links, a holdover from my father's days in the Ethiopian government, had the old Ethiopian flag with the Lion of Judah and his crooked crown on it. They were the only things of my father I had left. He used to keep them in a small gray jewelry box with the lid open on top of the dresser in his bedroom, although I can't remember ever having seen him wear them. What I can remember is him holding them out to me and saying with a slight, sarcastic lilt to his voice, "Someday all this will be yours." I don't think he ever actually intended for them to become heirlooms. They were just cheap cuff links from an old, decaying regime, but you hold on to what you can and hope the meaning comes later.

Before leaving the house I stood in front of my bathroom mirror and practiced my introduction. I brushed forward the edges of my thinning hair and patted down the sides of my small Afro. My reflection stared back disapprovingly. I had aged, but there was nothing distinguished about me. The laugh lines around my mouth had burrowed in, and there was more of my forehead than I cared to show. I smiled and tried to find a hint of a younger and better version of myself, but there was no doing. He was gone.

I stepped back from the mirror and practiced my introduction. I wanted to be ready for the moment Judith opened the door and found me standing on her steps. I wanted to strike the right chord, leave no room for error.

"Hello. Great to see you."

"I'm honored to be here. Thank you for having me."

"It's a pleasure to be here. It was so kind of you to invite me."

I tried to take my time walking to Judith's house, but all I had were two flights of stairs, two porches, and a few feet of sidewalk to separate us. I took the steps slowly. When I reached my front door I still had nine minutes to pass, so I tied and untied my shoelaces in front of my house. I looked up at the sky to see if there were any stars that I could count, or a moon to describe, but there was nothing, only clouds that still retained a muted shade of pink left from the sun.

When I finally rang the doorbell, Naomi answered. Her mother had tried to braid her hair into a row of plaits, but it had come out as a half-dozen uneven, lopsided braids that erupted into a tuft in the back. It gave Naomi an oddly menacing look that somehow seemed intended. She stood in the doorway looking like a lunatic and stared at me as if I were the man responsible for all of the world's frustrated desires, a fool who accidentally gave bad directions to people on their honeymoons, contemptuous but good-natured.

"You're late," she said.

I looked down at my watch. I was still five minutes early.

"I'm sorry, madame," I said, bowing my head just slightly. "But my chauffeur had a terrible time finding the house. I would fire him, but he is after all just a monkey, and you know how they can be."

"Henry?"

"Yes. How did you know?"

She shook her head, as if to say I *understand, more than you can ever imagine, just how difficult a monkey chauffeur can be.* This was not, of course, the only time I had pinned something on a monkey.

"My mom said you should wait in the living room," Naomi said.

She turned and darted up the stairs two at a time. As she did, the braids in the back of her hair bounced off her billowy Afro.

This was the first time I had ever been in Judith's living room, although I had seen fractions of it dozens of times before. At night, the heavy red curtains that draped over the front windows were pulled back far enough to allow more than a peek into the living room. It was the same thing with all of the other newly refurbished houses in the neighborhood; curtains provocatively peeled back to reveal a warmly lit room with forest green couches, modern silver lamps that craned their necks like swans, and sleek glass coffee tables with fresh flowers bursting on top. There was something about affluence that needed exposure, that resisted closed windows and poor lighting and made a willing spectacle of everything. The houses invited, practically begged and demanded, to be watched. When I took my walks at night, this was what I did. I stared into the living rooms of others. I stood across the street on the tips of my toes and tried to catch a glimpse of the kitchen, or the dining room, or the paintings on the wall. Kandinsky and Rothko prints over the sealed-up marble fireplaces; long, elegant dining tables made to look as if they had been hand-carved out of a single block of wood; walls that were painted a subtle shade of gold that was perhaps picked up by the massive vase of plastic sunflowers in the corner. Rarely did I ever see the people who lived in those houses, as if each were merely display-case props of revitalization. Sometimes I thought of what I was doing as window shopping.

An old record player and radio the size of a desk, made of wood and with a dozen chrome knobs, sat in the hallway. The living room had a heavy black wall-mounted phone from the early twentieth century, and a silver clock stuck permanently on two-twenty. The leather couches, chestnut colored and densely packed, were separated by a wooden coffee table that had at least fifty small drawers along its side. It was all so solid, comfortable, and familiar, as if Judith had deliberately picked only pieces of furniture that had proven their ability to withstand time.

From somewhere in the house, Judith called out, "I'll be right down. I just have to finish something up." Behind her voice I could hear Naomi's barely restrained cries to be left alone. In one of those rooms upstairs, Judith was pulling away at her daughter's hair, while her daughter was pulling away from her mother's confused, desperate hands. It was a subtle negotiation of unspoken differences.

When the two of them came down the stairs fifteen minutes later, each looked spent and frustrated. Naomi's hair was now all in braids, more or less evenly separated. She led the way, with her mother just a step behind. Judith was wearing her glasses, which gave her small, narrow face an added sense of depth that seemed to be previously missing.

"I'm sorry we kept you waiting so long. Naomi and I had some unfinished business to settle."

We kissed each other on both cheeks. Judith's hand lingered for what I thought was a second beyond polite on my back.

"You're the first dinner guest we've had in our new house."

"Well, I feel honored."

"You should. Naomi hates having other people in the house."

"Is that true, Naomi?"

Naomi was standing pressed against the wall with her hands tucked behind her.

"Yup," she said.

She popped her lips hard on the "p" for emphasis as she rocked back on her heels.

"You've got good taste for someone your age," I told her.

Judith led me to the dining room, which was still overrun with boxes of books that she said she didn't know what to do with. Most of them, she said, were terribly boring academic books that she didn't want to think about or look at anymore. In another life, she had been a professor of American political history.

"And for a while, it was great," she said. "I loved it. The students, the summers off. I could pick Naomi up from school every day. And at night I still had the energy to go out for dinner or watch a movie."

"What happened?" I asked her.

"I'm not sure," she said. "That life seems so far away now. Naomi's father left. That didn't help. We moved from Chicago to Boston to Virginia, and now here. Nothing felt good enough anymore."

She had the habit of tucking and untucking her hair from behind her right ear as she spoke. She hesitated for a few seconds before speaking again.

"Suddenly I saw myself twenty years in the future saying the same thing over and over to students who stayed the same age, and I couldn't believe that this was what I had planned on. It's hard sometimes to remember why we do anything in the first place. It's nice to think there's a purpose, or even a real decision that turns everything in one direction, but that's not always true, is it? We just fall into our lives. How did you get to own a grocery store?"

"Some people are just lucky," I said.

"Is that what that was?"

"It also helps if you don't care where you land."

Instead of sitting at the dining-room table, Judith suggested we eat on the couch.

"We can be less formal that way, don't you think?" she said.

I nodded my head in agreement. We ate our dinner off porcelain plates with gold-trimmed edges while sitting on the leather couches. Judith and Naomi were spread out on one while I sat across from them with my food delicately balanced on my lap. I watched every bite as it traveled from the tip of my fork into my mouth. I tried to erase any sound of food being ground into bits by chewing slowly, but it was never quite enough. I was still there, with all of my flaws, in Judith's immaculate living room, which was larger and grander than anything I had ever sat and eaten in since coming to Logan Circle. I kept my legs close together and limited my movements to a few simple nods of the head. My plate teetered on a few occasions, and had it fallen on the newly restored hardwood floors, I'm confident I would have shattered with it.

We ate in silence for several minutes, the only sounds being those of our forks scraping gently against the plates. Finally Judith made a desperate attempt to overcome the sudden silence.

"Did you ever get to read Ralph Emerson or Alexis de Tocqueville?" she asked.

"A little," I said.

"Years ago," I added a moment later to cover up the lie.

"Americans hate history," she said. She began to lecture then about Emerson and Tocqueville, about America's repudiation of history and its antipathy toward anything that resembled the past. Her eyes trailed off to a corner of the living room, where they stayed locked. She spoke eloquently and passionlessly, her words probably repeated a hundred times over the years in front of crowded classrooms. She wasn't speaking to me or Naomi but to the room, which needed to be filled with at least one of our voices. I nodded my head and listened attentively, trying to find a narrow gap in which I could insert a well-timed grunt of agreement.

"We always want to believe that we're the first to do anything," she continued. "We're always racing something or someone, even if it's all just in our head. We raced across America to get to the Pacific, and then we raced to build a railroad to connect it all. We raced to the moon. We raced to build as many bombs as was humanly possible. I wonder if now we haven't run out of things to race against. I think the moment that happens, we'll have nothing to do but look back. Then we'll know if it was worth it."

Naomi was leaning against her mother's legs, which were folded up on the couch specifically for that purpose. She was bored and staring at her fingernails. She chewed on the corner of her index finger while Judith talked. I wondered how many times she had heard this before, if she could repeat it word for word if asked.

"I should have taught a class called 'Races.' It could have been great."

"It's still not too late," I added.

"No. It is. I have a year-long sabbatical that I'm already halfway through and I can't see myself going back."

Naomi, who hadn't spoken throughout Judith's condensed lecture, finally found an opening to jump in.

"You should get a job," she said. "You could work at the store with Mr. Stephanos."

"But then what would he do?"

"He could watch me."

Judith leaned over her knees and wrapped her arms around Naomi's neck. I tried to look away as she did but instead caught her eyes staring at me from the side. It was my first victory of the evening.

"That doesn't sound too bad to me," I said.

After dinner Judith offered me a tour of the house while Naomi prepared for bed.

"It was amazing what this place looked like when I bought it. Parts of the floor were missing; most of the paint had fallen off; almost every window had a crack in it."

Every floor of the house had been meticulously restored. The second had been turned into a bedroom for Naomi, and a massive library and TV room; the first, into the living room and dining room we had just left. It was just as the construction workers had said. There were sliding doors over the built-in bookshelves that lined the walls, and on every floor there was a bathroom.

"They're for Naomi," she said. We were on the top floor, and Judith had just pointed to the fourth and last bathroom.

"We used to have these terrible fights. They only got worse after her father left. She hated both of us for that, but I was the only one around for her to take it out on, which made her hate me even more. We would fight and she would lock herself in one of the bedrooms for hours at a time. There was nothing I could do to get her out. A couple of times I left her alone and she ended up running away from the house. She never went far. I actually found her once in a closet right by the front door. But still, I always went mad trying to find her. I pictured her hurt or kidnapped, or some other awful thought that I couldn't fight back, and I would take off running, but I guess you already know that part.

"I made a promise to her when we moved here. I told her she could have all the space she wanted. In return, she had to promise to stop running out of the house when she got upset. Now, when she gets mad, she can lock herself on any floor of the house and never have to worry about seeing me, or anyone else."

She smiled, and then laughed a little, holding her hand to her mouth.

"I know this sounds ridiculous. But it works, most of the time, and right now that's all I really care about. This is our third house in as many years, and if it took a half-dozen bathrooms and as many floors to make it work, that's what I would have done."

I couldn't help but admire Judith's devotion to her daughter, precisely because of its excesses. Who didn't want to be loved like that? She didn't apologize for anything, and I believed her completely when she said she would have built half a dozen bathrooms if needed. But it wasn't just because she wanted to make Naomi happy. All you had to do was look at her eyes for a few minutes to see how tired and full of regret she was. She wanted peace; a hundred extra feet of plumbing were surely worth that.

"This must sound ridiculous to you," she said.

"Nope," I said. I popped my "p" just as hard, if not harder, than Naomi had done earlier. It was a silly thing to have done, but it made Judith laugh with relief, which was more than I could have hoped for. This time, instead of covering her mouth with her hand, she stretched out her fingers and without think-ing took two of mine in hers. She leaned in just far enough for me to meet her face less than halfway. It wasn't a kiss so much as it was a gentle press, or an extended graze of lips, full of a sud-den, almost crushing tenderness. We held it for as long as we could, three, maybe four seconds at most, and then the moment passed.

Judith took a slight step back and said, "I should go check on Naomi."

"It must be getting late," I said.

"I'll walk you to the door," she said.

She walked me to the door and leaned her head outside so she could see my building.

"Get home safely," she said.

"I'll try."

Less than a minute later and I was climbing the steps to my own apartment. There hadn't been enough space between her house and mine for me to linger over the evening. Within a few minutes I was struggling to fit my key into my door, since the light on the landing had burned out months ago and no one had ever thought of replacing it, and then I was turning the knob and leaning into the door, which always creaked as if it were about to fall off its hinges. When I turned the living-room light on and stared into my apartment, an inevitable sense of regret swept over me. How much better would it have been to have spent even just a few minutes walking in the cold? Or to have sat on the stairwell in the pitch black, unable to see my hand in front of my face? There I could have replayed pieces of our conversation, reenacted our gestures, imagined alternatives. In the harsh light of my apartment, there was only room for practical concerns. The en-tire place was shabbier, smaller, and more desolate than I remembered, as if while I was eating dinner someone had entered my apartment and stolen a few years off the furniture. The only thing that wasn't scavenged from the trash was a solid oak desk that I had saved for three months to buy. Everything else bore the stamp of too many lives and too many people. The couch was draped with a heavy navy blue fabric I had bought from a garment store to cover up the unknown stains and worn armrests. The coffee table was balanced by a stack of magazines on one side and an old bowl on the other. The rug in the center of the room had been left by the previous tenant, who had most likely inherited it from the tenant before him. The ends were so frayed that at least twice a month I had to trim a piece off to keep from tripping on the loops of extended thread. Five years later now and one end of the rug was noticeably longer than the other; the corners had been rounded off, and then cut like a pie sliced into at odd, uneven angles. The television had knob dials and terrible reception, and it sat on an old trunk that looked solid from a distance, but was in fact practically paper thin. A man, I told myself, is defined not by his possessions but by the company he keeps. That was a phrase I had stolen from my father, along with this: the character of a man is like the tail of a monkey; it is always behind him. I knew from experience that moments of sorrow and self-pity were the best times to think of these old phrases and axioms. Not because they provided any comfort, but because, like any other deliberate act of memory, they could supplant the present with their own incorrigible truth.

From my living-room window I could see the lights in Judith's house. There was at least one room on every floor that was fully lit. I decided there was something monstrous about a house with so many lights, something distinctly unjust.

After I'd been standing there for only a few minutes, the lights on the second floor began to flicker on and off. It was a signal from Naomi. We began to turn our lights off and on in an imaginary Morse code dialogue. I could picture her standing by the switch, eagerly flicking the lights until her head began to hurt. Finally, instead of continuing to respond, I just stood in the dark and tried not to think of her disappointment.

☙

The next day Joseph and Kenneth came to the store and I told them about my dinner with Judith. I had mentioned her before—the house, Naomi, our conversations at the store—but only infrequently, and with no more passion than I discussed anything else that might have happened on that given day. When I told them about the dinner and brief kiss, the two of them looked up from their chessboard at each other, and not me.

"You see?" Joseph said. "You should listen to me more often." He was wagging one of his chubby fingers at Kenneth, who was now leaning back in his chair with his hands folded on his stomach.

"What can I say? You were right."

"About what?" I asked.

"Jo-Jo said you were . . .what's the word you used?"

"Enamored."

"Yes. Enamored by this woman."

When I looked over at Joseph he was struggling and failing to contain his grin.

"You have nothing to be embarrassed about, Stephanos. You've been in America for almost seventeen years. It's about time you dated a white woman."

"I hadn't thought of it that way."

"He's right," Kenneth jumped in. "You spend too much time

by yourself. You're in this store all alone, and then you go home. It's no way for a man to live."

"What about the little girl's father?" Joseph asked me.

"It was just dinner," I said.

"Where is he?"

"I don't know. I've never asked her."

"I imagine if I saw the three of you walking down the street, I would think you were it."

There was a second of silence before Kenneth reached across the table and smacked Joseph on the arm.

"Sorry, Stephanos. You know what I meant."

"Of course," I told him.

Joseph won the chess game easily, as he always did. Whenever he plays against Kenneth or me, he does so absentmindedly, his fingers dancing over the board as if he were seeing it for the first time. When he moves a piece, he never focuses on the spot he's moving it to. Instead, he turns his eyes back to his opponent, or even better, to someone else in the room, lending an air of inevitability to every move he makes. As a young man, he had been one of the better chess players in Kinshasa, known for his quiet, restrained demeanor even in the face of certain defeat. He had stories of all-night chess tournaments held in dingy cafés and bars, games that erupted into beatings, stabbings, and on occasion, shootings. "We had no jobs, we were done with school, no family, no money, so we played chess all day. It was what we did." Clusters, and in some cases, surrogate families of young men formed around the game. Some were illiterate and had spent years fighting from the bush; others, like Joseph, were born into affluent families who had paid for French and English tutors before losing everything to Mobutu and his corrupt, bloated government. They had a religious devotion to the game, a respect for its handful of rules and almost infinite variations born, as Joseph said, out of a shared sense of gratitude for having at least one space where their decisions mattered. "Nobody," he said once, "understands chess like an African."

After the game was over, Joseph settled back into a quiet contemplation that involved deep breaths and long pauses between each sip of beer. Winning these games gave him nothing. Kenneth was rearranging the pieces on the board, trying to discover where he had gone wrong. If and when he figured it out, he would rock back in his chair and exclaim, "Now I see what you did, you tricky bastard. That will never work again with me."

"You know," Joseph said to me, "I dated a white woman once. She was from Boston. She had short curly red hair, so the teachers nicknamed her Rouge."

"When?" I asked him.

"A long time ago."

"In the Congo?"

"In Zaire. She was a Peace Corps volunteer."

"For how long?"

"Almost two years."

"You didn't waste any time, did you?"

"What can I say? It was meant to be. We were teaching at the same school."

"And then what?"

"She went back to Boston."

"And you lost touch?"

"We never tried to keep it. Maybe I wrote her a letter once or twice, but nothing more than that. We had talked briefly about getting married and having little red Afro babies together, but we both knew better. She lives here now. I see her every once in a while. She's come into the restaurant a few times for lunch."

"What do you say to her?"

"Nothing."

"Not even once?"

"I don't think she recognizes me."

"How could she not?" I asked him.

He finished his beer and patted his stomach.

"I was skinnier then," he said. "You should have seen me. I was so beautiful. You wouldn't have believed your eyes."

5

On May 4 I wake up earlier than usual with my head still clouded from last night's drinking. The sun has barely cracked through the day, and I can still hear Joseph's voice singing in the bar. As I swing my legs onto the floor, I make a firm resolution to myself. To go on living halfheartedly is ridiculous, I think. Here I am; this is it. Starting today, I am going to press on valiantly. I am going to march through the hours and weeks and let no disappointment, regardless of how large, steer me from my course or bring me down. I am going to open my store early. I am going to catch the morning rush-hour commuters and make them mine.

By seven a.m. I'm fully dressed and walking out the door. Five minutes later, I'm standing in front of my store, pulling the keys out of my pocket. All around me people are walking, rushing, and for the first time since Judith and Naomi left the neighborhood,

I am one of them. The morning is bright and mild; it is a picture-perfect May day with low humidity and surges of cool air that dry the sweat on my forehead as quickly as it forms. The day, I tell myself, is nothing to be afraid of. Life ticks on just as it always has. It was only by a trick of the imagination that I had come to believe I could step outside of it. Sunlight is tilting through the space between the leaves, lighting up the edges of the circle nearest my store. The sight is so perfect that I pause for a second, keys in hand, with the deliberate intention of admiring it.

I lift the lock from its latch, grab hold of the lowest rung on the grate, and with three quick, solid jerks hurl it over my head and send it crashing. That same sound is echoing from stores all across this city; it is we, the small storekeepers and newspaper vendors, who are drawing it back to life.

The grate crashes and locks into place, and as it does, a thin white envelope, slid into a corner of the door, flutters to the ground. My name is typed neatly on the front, with no postage or address. I pick it up and hold it against the sky. The sun catches it from the back. Through the envelope I can make out one clear line: *Dear Mr. Stephanos.*

Dear Mr. Stephanos. My knees give, just a bit, at the sight of the words. Something—call it hope, optimism—drops in my stomach and goes running. *Dear Mr. Stephanos.* A sign of official business. Never in my life have I done well with official business. Official business is prompt and efficient and demanding. I have a stack of official letters from vendors and utility companies and a credit card that all begin the same way: *Dear Mr. Stephanos.* In each of them there is a simple, unwavering demand for money, for which I've had no response except to close my eyes and wish desperately like a child that it would all go away. I have done the best I can under the circumstances. I write out checks

THE BEAUTIFUL THINGS THAT HEAVEN BEARS

for meager amounts: $10.34 here, $3.29 there. And when I can't, I have learned not to pick up my phone or read my mail for a week or two at a time.

I bring the letter with me into the store. I don't turn on the lights or lift the blinds. With the exception of the lifted grate, there is no sign that I am open for business. No one, I notice, even bothers to slow down or look in.

I lock the door behind me and place the letter on the counter. I turn it over once, and then twice. Courage, my father used to say, is being able to face the truth, regardless of what it may be, and remembering that, I tear the letter open along the side and take the kind of deep breath that's supposed to brace you for bad news. I begin at the top of the page.

From the law firm of Elkin and Govind to Mr. Sepha Stephanos.

The name of the firm is familiar. I've seen it before on bus ad-vertisements and on daytime television commercials. I can't de-cide whether receiving a letter from a firm that advertises on plastic place cards to a captive audience makes the situation even worse. I never expected to be on the receiving end of a letter from a law firm that uses people lying in hospital beds as part of their advertising campaign, but life can be cruel and unpredictable, which is precisely what such firms are there to remind us of.

Beneath the letterhead is a date, May 3. The letter must have been left on my door sometime during the previous night while Joseph, Kenneth, and I were staring shyly at naked women.

Dear Mr. Stephanos:
   This letter is to inform you that you have thirty days to vacate the property at 1150 P Street, NW, Washington, D.C. 20008.

There are no treacherous demands or insinuating threats. The words become simple black characters against a page. Each character forms a word as discrete from the next as two strangers in a room. The letter is almost a page long, and mentions, in brief detail, my long history of overdue rent payments, going back ten years to a time when a few late months meant nothing in a neighborhood where each cleared check was cause enough for celebration and wonder. The tide has turned since then, and I have failed to keep pace. I could ask how this happened, but I know that I have no right to be surprised or angry. It's May and I have yet to pay the rent for February, March, or April. I have let the store go; the aisles are once again burdened with sagging shelves, and somewhere in the back of the refrigerator cartons of milk are solidifying. It wasn't supposed to have been like this. There was supposed to have been a string of good months. I had seen moving trucks with gilded mirrors and plush couches. There were construction workers who came to my store for lunch every day. I had a brand-new deli counter. I was supposed to have done so much by now. I was to have expanded my store into something bigger, grander, like a lunch counter, a grocery store, or a restaurant that people would take pride in. A place that I could truthfully write letters home about. I have learned to be a modest man, and never to exceed my means, but even poor men are allowed dreams from time to time. Who can blame me for this? No one can. I deserved it all.

I take a stand at the counter, on the opposite side of the register, and run my hand over the dusty white Formica top. Every story has an ending, and this letter, I realize, is going to be the shape of mine.

"This is no longer my store."

When I need to convince myself of something, I say it out

loud. This has been a habit of mine since childhood, something that I have always needed to do to align my thoughts with reality.

I shorten the phrase to make it more declarative before I say it again.

"This is not my store. This is not my counter, and that is not my register."

What I want is to pick up each and every item in the store, run my hand along the walls and even the floor, over every piece of tile and packaged good, and repeat my negation of it.

I read the letter two, and then three times, and a few more times after that for good measure. It's printed out on a nice piece of letterhead that has type in two different colors. I call Kenneth at work to tell him what's happening. He answers on the first ring. I read him the opening sentence, and then ramble on about inflated rents, slow months, and lines of credit still owed. I try to sound indignant, or at least angry, but I know that instead my voice comes across as lost, perhaps even childish. Kenneth is silent for a long time before he says anything.

"Isn't this what you wanted?" he finally asks.

"I never said that."

"No. That's true. You never said, 'I want to open and close my store whenever I want, lose all my customers, and then be forced out of business.' But that doesn't mean you didn't want it."

"I didn't want it."

"Then why haven't you done something, Stephanos?"

His voice is full of pity when he says that last line. I know if he had thought saying it would have done any good, he would have encouraged me with all the pep and enthusiasm of a high school football coach. As it is, his disappointment is greater than mine.

"I will. You're right. I'll figure something out."

"I don't have that kind of money, but—"

I know what he wants to say next, but I won't let him.

"Joseph Kony," I say.

"What?"

"Joseph Kony."

A few seconds of silence passes before he says anything else. In that time, I twirl the phone cord around my index finger so tightly I can see the blood swelling at the tip.

"Uganda. The Lord's Resistance Army. The L.R.A.," he says.

"Easy enough," I tell him.

"He likes to mutilate children. Chops off their ears and lips and nose. He says he can speak to angels."

"Very precise."

"I'm an engineer. Plus we did this before."

"I don't remember."

"We did it backwards. We began with the L.R.A. It was one of Joseph's."

Before he can say anything else, I tell him I'll see him Tuesday, and hang up the phone. I don't know why I didn't call Joseph first. Joseph, with his half-drunk glasses of wine and tattered University of Michigan sweatshirt, would have understood.

Rather than immediately open the store, I take the stool that Naomi used to sit on and place it in front of the door. I climb on top and look out, taking stock of all I see. There are water stains on the ceiling. In the back corner, the paint is once again slowly peeling toward the door. I count twenty-three pieces of tile that need to be replaced. The shelves on the right-hand wall need to be replaced. There are eggs rotting in the back of the refrigerator. Expired packages of bread are crowded together in the second aisle. A thick layer of dust hangs over the paper towels, toilet paper, and diapers that sit on the top shelf. On the left-hand wall sits a stack of school supplies: notebooks, crayons, folders, looseleaf paper, pens and pencils and scissors that I can't even remember ordering, much less selling. A quarter of one aisle is reserved for beauty supplies—hair gel, relaxer kits, shower caps—that I got conned into buying by Mrs. Davis's nephew. There's a rotating rack of old comic books near the door. Calendars from 1993, 1994, and 1996 are still hanging on the wall behind the counter. The cash register is cracked along the side. The bulletproof windowpanes I had put in four months ago are barely thick enough to stop a kid with a decent arm and a rock in his hand. I still sell Bubble Tape bubble gum, and as far I know, I'm the only store in the neighborhood to do so. I remember that there's a case of Tab soda in the basement. I love the things that are timeless: detergent, paper products, toys, Hostess cupcakes, scissors, rolls of tape, Wite-Out, hair gel, soap, nightcaps, anything made of plastic—the things that endure and survive.

It's almost eleven by the time I finally open the store and let in the first customers of the day, a pair of tourists: husband and wife, white, thin, and well dressed, with hair graying elegantly from the front to the back. They're on a self-guided walking tour of D.C., the kind that involves enormous fold-up maps, fanny packs, and little Did You Know quizzes with check boxes on the side. They wander through the store for a few minutes, finally settling on two cans of soda and a pack of cinnamon gum. The man puts one hand on the counter and leans back.

"There are some beautiful old houses around here," he says. He speaks with an assured, confident authority that I envy. I agree. I tell him that a president's uncle or cousin used to live in one of them, along with some senators and congressmen from a different era.

"Did you know," I ask him, "that this was once one of the most desirable neighborhoods in the city? You had to have connections to live here, money, power. It was that sort of place."

He's impressed, as if somehow this information confirmed something not only about the neighborhood, but himself as well. I ramble on and tell them what I know about General Logan.

"General John A. Logan," I tell them, "was a Civil War hero. He fought at Bull Run and Vicksburg," all information that can be found on Logan's pedestal.

"Perhaps his greatest achievement in the war," I add, "was that he saved Raleigh, North Carolina, from being burned to the ground." This I have only recently learned. It has since become my favorite historical fact regarding General Logan.

"He was a great man," I add, as if somehow it isn't enough to merely recount Logan's virtues, or to simply point toward the statue in the center of the circle. What I want is for him to be a hero to us all.

The man touches the brim of his hat as he leaves. His wife smiles and nods. I watch them as they walk out of the store into the bright, sunny spring morning still touched by an occasional cool breeze. The city is bursting. The old, wide, boulevard-like roads and L'Enfant's once practical, now useless circles are growing heavy with the weight of spring and summer. Tree branches and bushes droop with fat white buds while hordes of weeds break through the dead grass. The couple cross the street and head toward the circle. They are not holding hands, but they are walking so close to each other that a part of their shoulders or arms is always touching. Their steps are perfectly in sync: after all their years together, they now have the same walk. I come out from behind the counter and stand in front of my store so I can watch them enter the circle and pause in front of General Logan's statue. The man pulls a book out of his fanny pack and steps up to the short metal fence that was recently put up to protect the grass around the base. They both crane their heads up so they can stare into the raised hoof of Logan's horse, suspended in midair, waiting to land triumphantly on whoever stands in its path.

A few moments later they unfold their map and look around at the street signs. The husband points west to P Street, which, along with Rhode Island Avenue, Vermont Avenue, and 13th Street, hits the circle like the spoke of a bicycle wheel. Of all the streets that meet the circle, P is by far my favorite. As it heads west toward Dupont and Georgetown, it only grows prettier and wider, with the houses increasingly grand and luxurious, as if each step forward were a step toward paradise. Men with matching dogs walk along P Street. Half a mile away are sidewalk cafés and restaurants, three used-book stores, wine shops, flower shops, and cheese shops. And the farther up P you move, the better life gets. From Dupont the street proceeds to Georgetown, where the road narrows and the sidewalks become a quaint uneven brick bordered by nineteenth-century colonial mansions bearing Ionic columns. The trees form a canopy over the cobblestone road, still lined with the metal tracks of the trolley cars that stopped running decades ago.

The wife nods her head, rubs her hand across her husband's back, and they begin to walk away from General Logan and his horse. As soon as I see them leaving the circle, I cross the street and begin to follow from a safe distance. Soon, without thinking about it, I'm across the street and jogging lightly to keep up with the couple, who are now just a few steps away from P Street. I cut through the circle to catch up with them, and when I hit General Logan's statue, I finally pause for a second and look back at my store. I can see it clearly from here, everything from the sagging right gutter to the streaks of blue paint along the side to the metal bars over the windows shining in the sun. How is it that in all these years, I've never seen my store look quite like this? I can imagine it wanting to be spared the burden of having to survive another year. The door is unlocked. The sign is flipped to "Open" and the cash register, with its contents totaling $3.28, is ajar. I wonder if this is what it feels like to walk out on your wife and children. If this is what it feels like to leave a car on the side of the highway and never come back for it. What is the proper equation, the perfect simile or metaphor? I'm an immigrant. I should know this. I've done it before.

I follow the couple to P Street, turning back toward my store one last time to give it a wave good-bye. I swing right onto P only half a block behind them. They have a slow, leisurely pace to their walk, perfect for the day, which is bright and growing warmer. With each new step we take, the world feels lighter and lighter.

The G2 bus grinds its way to a stop in front of us. A group of older black women get off and cross the street to catch the bus back in the opposite direction. They shake their heads, lost. I imagine them doing this all day and night, traveling back and forth to the edge of the known world only to return, in the end, to the broken neighborhood they had just left. At 14th Street the narrow seclusion of P intersects with the wide-open thorough-fare that runs almost the entire length of the city. Just a few months ago there was a liquor store and a Chinese carryout restaurant on the corner, Yum's Chinese and Chicken. It was the first place I ate at alone in D.C. I walked in early in the evening and ordered a beef and broccoli that I ate while standing on the corner. I was nineteen, and had been in America for less than forty-eight hours. I remember being asked for spare change every few minutes by the same man, the red neon glare from the 7-Eleven across the street, and the roaming bands of kids who swaggered by. The food tasted like a sweet soy sauce that, whenever I've come across it again, instantly brings me back to that corner and night.

We cross 14th and watch as the neighborhood grows nicer. Skinny new trees have been planted along the sidewalk. Yum's, or "Yu s," as the sign now reads, is gone, and so is the liquor store. They have obediently made way for newer and better things, whatever they may eventually be. I can't say that I particularly liked either of them, but that's beside the point. Now that they are gone I can begin to miss them with a sentimental fondness I could have never mustered otherwise. Newspapers cover the windows of both storefronts, along with a sign that vaguely reads "Coming Soon."

There are town homes being built on the left and a two-story organic grocery store being built on the right. Before all of this there was an abandoned lot with an eight-foot barbed-wire fence and a three-foot hole in the center, a grocery store that sold wilted vegetables and grade-D meat, an auto repair shop, and a black-owned bookstore called Madame X. On a warm night, you could buy a blowjob or any number of drugs there, depending on your mood. You could walk by and catch the disinterested stare of a woman leaning against the fence out of the corner of your eye and see men slumped on the ground, their heads lolling obliviously to the side. In the morning and after school, children scoured the weed-filled grounds looking for money that might have fallen out of someone's pocket. What they found they used to buy candy and chips from my store. At Madame X, the black empowerment books gathered dust, the occasional scent of weed wafted out the door, and on Thursday nights you could sit in on an open-mike reading and share in the plate of yam patties passed around the room. The rotting meat at the grocery store next door was discounted further at the end of every week and sold with new expiration dates. Occasionally someone complained and threatened a boycott, and for a week or month the aisles were marginally but noticeably cleaner, the meat a little fresher. Stolen cars were driven into the auto repair shop at night and came out in the morning with new coats of paint and fresh license plates. Had you known this stretch of P Street back then, you would have agreed that it was a hell of a block.

By 15th Street the trees are fully grown. Massive elms and oaks shade the gray-and-white four-story row houses. On opposite sides of the corner sit two hulking gray temples. The wife stops at the corner and pulls out her guidebook. She shakes her head and points north. They march on one block farther until they reach the corner of 16th and P. You can see the White House from here. The street unfurls from its gate like a massive concrete carpet rolling straight for several blocks before dipping into a tunnel and rising up once again. I used to think that there was some great metaphor in this. I used to walk to this very corner after I closed the store so I could watch the cars, buses, and people head toward the White House as if that alone was their final destination. A slow day or bad week didn't matter as much then, not as long as I could believe, however foolishly, that just a stone's throw away was a higher power that I could appeal to. I imagined all of those people clamoring to get into the Oval Office, where the president sat waiting to hear their complaints and woes, their solutions and ideas. A great Santa Claus and father for adults.

I watch the couple as they pause at the corner and the husband points south to the White House. I can hear him saying, "That is where our president lives." For some, it's still enough to walk up to the metal gates and south lawn and gaze into the halls of greatness.

Spring is riding high on 17th. The sidewalks are crowded with outdoor seating. The men are holding hands and kissing each other gently on the lips. The bolder ones are already wearing tank tops and black spandex shorts. There's a scent to the air here that you can't find anywhere else in the city. A mixture of fresh sweat, blooming flowers, and coffee. I want to take the couple gently by the hand and lead them down the street to Samuel's café, where we could sit under the green awning on a busy corner and watch the crowd. This, I would tell them, is all I want out of life, to sit here on these plastic lawn chairs and watch the parade of skinny and muscular men, old and young, as they flirt and fight with each other. Joseph loves it here as well. He says it reminds him of France, with the cafés, the air, and the pretty boys with nothing to do. According to him, "It's the only civilized place in the city." I caught him here once, standing drunk against a light post, his hands tucked deep into his pockets, a scarf flung around his neck. It was early in the evening, before the sun had set, and he was watching the procession with a distant, nostalgic look spread over his face. This was as close as he was going to get to that better life, the one that had him stomping through the streets of Paris with the perfect French phrase waiting on the tip of his tongue. I didn't say anything to him. I just watched him from across the street as he nodded his head, stamped his feet to a song blaring from a moving car.

Dupont Circle is only a few blocks ahead. I can see from here that the white marble fountain in the center has been turned on. A fine mist spread by the breeze is spraying the people sitting on its edge. Admiral du Pont would have been proud to have this scene named in his honor. The office buildings are clearing out for lunch. People are taking their food outside, picnicking on the fresh grass that surrounds the outer perimeter of the circle. Almost everyone is dressed casually. Some people are lying on the grass with a book suspended in front of them. No harm can happen here. The man and woman join hands as they cross the street and enter the circle. I've begun to think of the couple as old friends whom I'm admiring from a distance. I can see their children, slightly estranged but still loving, and their home, a split-level ranch in the suburbs of some midsize city: St. Louis, Kansas City, or Tulsa. The wife has a habit of lifting her arms too high as she walks, as if at any moment she's ready to break into a sprint. Occasionally her husband catches her by the elbow and settles her arm into place. I wonder what this means. I picture early-morning power walks in matching Nike track suits, frequent visits to the doctor that always end in disappointing news, blood pressure medication, a daily aspirin and glass of red wine. "Breathe," he tells her.

Together, we walk around the fountain twice. A spot opens up on one of the benches surrounding the fountain. A few feet away, I can see a clearing in the grass. The couple turn toward the bench, while I head toward the grass. I give them an enthusiastic wave good-bye as we part.

6

The morning after my dinner at Judith's house, I waited anxiously in my store for her to come in. I had prepared myself for anything from a warm, deep embrace to a casual, indifferent air that said all too plainly not to expect more than just that one brief kiss. I kept the invitation that Naomi had folded up and left in my mailbox buried in my pocket. I rubbed my fingers across it from time to time, and with each rub I came to a new conclusion: that the kiss was merely an accident; that the kiss meant nothing; that the kiss had been deliberate and planned. Judith didn't come to the store that day, though, and neither did Naomi. When I closed the grates at the end of the night, I did so feeling dejected and suddenly abandoned. I told myself that I had no right to expect more, but that was hardly consoling when in fact more was precisely what I wanted.

The next day was even worse. I turned my abandonment into

anger and my anger into pity. I cursed myself for my silly expectations. I thought I saw the situation now clearly for what it
was—a case of mistaken identity. I had forgotten who I was,
with my shabby apartment and run-down store, and like any
great fool, I had tried to recast myself into the type of man who
dined casually on porcelain plates and chatted easily about Emerson and Tocqueville while sitting on a plush leather couch in a
grand house. The second day passed and still there was no sign
of either Judith or Naomi. I lay awake in bed and vowed to forget that night had ever happened.

I didn't have to wait long to test my resolve. The following
evening I saw Judith, by chance, as she walked up the steps of her
house. I was less than a block away when I saw her, and instinctively I began to rush toward her, ready at any moment to yell
out her name. I had covered half the distance separating us when
I saw Mrs. Davis standing in front of our house, cocooned from
head to toe in a blue coat, watching me as I nearly ran to catch
up with Judith before she vanished into her home. I slowed down
as soon as I saw Mrs. Davis watching me. I took a deep breath
and silently exhaled Judith's name. Had I been saved from making a fool of myself? Perhaps. I didn't need Mrs. Davis or anyone
else to tell me what I looked like chasing after Judith as she
walked up the steps of her house. I knew that already, and yet
still there it was, regret, fully formed and ready to wash over me
as soon as I realized that I wasn't going to take one more step.

Abruptly, I stopped walking and fixed myself into a square
patch of concrete that forced the crowd of people around me to
split as they approached. From there, I watched as Judith fumbled through her purse for keys. I noticed that at that moment,
she lost all of the grace with which she usually carried herself.
She could have been anybody, I told myself. She could have been

a stranger. Both of her hands scrambled desperately through her purse, which was large and heavy enough to throw her slightly off balance. It was cold outside and her frustration was visible even from where I was standing. She had no gloves on and her fingers must have stung with every stab she made. I knew enough about Judith to know that she carried as much of her life with her as possible everywhere she went. She had shown me the contents of her purse once while she was in the store searching for loose change to pay for a package of gum.

"Look at this purse," she had said. "I feel like a maniac carrying it around, but I don't know what I'd do without it."

Her purse was stuffed with utility bills, checks, credit cards, passport, keys to her old houses in Chicago and Virginia, a copy of Naomi's birth certificate and Social Security card along with her daughter's most recent report cards and immunization forms, everything one could ever need to assert her identity and place in the world. There was something sinister and romantic to it. Part fugitive, part adventurer, she was always ready to drop everything and run on a dime.

By the time she found her keys the people who passed me on the street had begun to turn around and stare back curiously at me. As they rushed home from the cold I had stood frozen in place for, what? Five, ten, fifteen minutes. Long enough to invite malicious and concerned glances. How was it that I never seemed to understand time when Judith was around? Too fast or too slow, or as in this case, not at all. An hour had sixty minutes and a minute had sixty seconds and the hour could be broken into halves and quarters and tenths and even fifths, and yet none of these parcels of time could be counted on to hold their weight at these moments. Judith disappeared into what I hoped was the warm comfort of her house with a slight nudge of her shoulder and a repositioning of her bag around the crook of her forearm. It was time for me to move on, but when I came to my house I didn't even pause to consider going in. I walked past it to the end of the corner, where instead of looping around the circle, I turned right onto Rhode Island Avenue—an unexpectedly wide and open road—and continued north until I reached a bar, where I stopped and drank until I knew everyone in the house next to mine had fallen asleep.

Three days later Judith rang my doorbell at just a few minutes past eleven. I had forgotten what my doorbell sounded like. I couldn't even remember the last time it had been pressed. When you live alone for as long as I have, you forget your private world is only an illusion created by a door and a key. The sound of the doorbell, harsh and sustained like the shrill cry of an old man, seemed capable of shattering all the windows and glass and tearing down the roof over my head if pressed long enough. When it rang my heart pressed against my chest and stayed there until I caught my breath and reordered the world to allow for such things as guests and doorbells.

Judith was patient with my coming down the steps. She pressed only once, knowing, perhaps from her bathroom-window view, that I was at home. As I came down the steps I could see her through the octagonal windowpanes on the front door. The dark orange streetlight added a touch of unexpected sadness to the scene. She was blowing into her hands for warmth, and behind her a few stray snow flurries drifted past. Do we plan encounters like this, or do they really just happen naturally? As I took the last few steps I thought of Bogart, with his dame-slapping ways, and the desperate women who came running to him at night.

When I opened the door Judith's back was turned to me, her

arms wrapped around her shoulders as she watched the falling snow. She wasn't wearing a coat. She was acting reckless. When she turned to face me she smiled wholeheartedly and pressed the palm of her hand against my face.

"Cold?" she asked.

"Freezing."

"Then invite me in."

We fumbled our way up the staircase, which grew darker as we neared the top floor. Before I opened the door I mumbled an apology about not expecting visitors and the general state of my apartment. I had cleaned it just the night before, but expectations are easier to bear when they're set as low as possible.

"I wish I had a coat to throw dramatically on the couch. It would fit the moment better, wouldn't it?" Judith had just cast a quick sidelong glance at the apartment, noting without apparent judgment the size and condition of the furniture and walls. It seemed enough for her that the place existed, that I indeed had the proverbial roof over my head and did not, despite my obvious isolation, live in a state of sordid squalor. It may very well have been relief that had crept into her voice and relaxed her enough to set us off on this game.

"I was just thinking the same thing," I said. "I could go to the closet and get you one."

"Can we start all over?"

"From outside?"

"No. That would be too much. I can just knock on the door."

I went to the closet and pulled out a long black wool coat that my uncle had given me for formal occasions. Judith held the coat up before putting it on and said, "Perfect." The shoulders, bulge, and length looked ridiculous and yet adorable on her. I could see how as a child she must have been equally precocious and charming, an entertaining little character who could be brought out in her mother's oversize clothes to amuse elderly aunts and grandparents.

Judith went into the landing and waited a few seconds before knocking on the door. When I opened it she blew right past me, flung the coat on the couch, and then collapsed onto it herself. She rested her forearm against her head and closed her eyes. It was a perfect performance.

Once the experience had settled in she asked, "So, how was that?"

"Better. Much better. Although I think a little dialogue at the door might have helped."

"Like what?"

"I don't know. 'Am I disturbing you?' 'Are you alone?' That sort of thing. How do you know, for instance, that I wasn't with another woman?"

"Or man."

"Exactly."

"I'll keep that in mind for next time. Anything else?"

"Where's Naomi?"

"Asleep."

"By herself?"

"Tylenol PM. It works wonders. I'm only kidding. All the doors are locked, though, including the one leading to the third floor. A mother can never be too careful."

She was slightly drunk. I saw that now. As she spoke, her head lolled unwittingly to the side, and her eyes, in the full glare of the hundred-watt ceiling bulbs, were heavily hooded.

"Is everything all right?" I asked her.

She paused for a second and fixed her eyes directly onto mine. I knew the technique. I had seen hundreds of parents do it before with their children in my store. The fixed, stern gaze against which any deceit was supposed to be helpless.

"Why didn't you say anything to me the other day?" she asked.

"When?"

"When I was standing in front of my door for God knows how long pretending I couldn't find my keys. You don't think I saw you standing down the block waiting for me to disappear?"

I didn't know what to tell her. She sat there and stared at me with that narrow doll-like head of hers that made her look as seemingly innocent as a child. I wanted to laugh the past six days off, and now that Judith was sitting here in my living room late on a winter evening, everything seemed entirely possible once again. I could fit into her life after all. There was nothing crazy about it. I had the trust and affection of her daughter, and once, not that long ago, I had been a young boy with the greatest ambitions and dreams, guided by a prominent father and distinguished family background. I still had that in me.

"I'm sorry," I said. "You looked like you were in a hurry and I didn't want to disturb you."

It wasn't much of an answer, but it was easier than the truth.

"Forget it," she said. "I'm just babbling."

My eyes followed hers from one corner to the next, catching sight of the spiderwebs hugging the northwest corner and the trail of dust creeping along the surfaces in a steady, unstoppable march.

"So this is it," she said.

"It's not much," I said.

"No. It's perfect. It's exactly as I imagined it. You have a great sense of space."

"You mean I don't have any furniture."

"That's just one way of looking at it. I always thought I would live a sparer life," she said. "I never wanted to be one of those people who had walls and walls of stuff they could care less about. I thought that would be the death of me."

"So what happened?"

"Inheritances. They can kill you."

She laughed just slightly at her joke without looking up to see if I had caught it.

"First it was my grandmother. Most of the furniture in the house came from her. Then there were a few aunts who had no children, a godmother in Boston who I barely even knew, and then finally my mother and father. I'm not sure what it is about me, but for some reason when people are about to die they seem to think of me. I think it's because they know I'll never throw any of it away."

She smoothed down the loose fabric of the sofa cushion that had puckered around her. It was a hideous couch, with green and red stripes and more than a few unknown stains. There wasn't a piece of furniture in my apartment that I wouldn't have traded in if given half a chance.

"You got anything to drink?" she asked me. "The scene wouldn't be complete if you didn't."

I pulled a bottle of expensive scotch that Kenneth had brought to the store and never finished from my kitchen cupboard. I had tried to finish the bottle alone on several occasions, but each time it had been obvious from the first glass that any comfort it was supposed to provide would elude me, and so now, four years later, the same half-drunk bottle was still gathering dust inside the cabinet.

"Stale scotch okay?" I asked her.

"I don't know what could possibly be better."

I set out two glasses and filled them partially with ice. This was a deliberate act of seduction; I had seen it before in television and movies. There was a direct chain of events that had to be followed: the glasses of scotch and ice led to the couch, which in turn led to the first hesitant kiss of the night, followed by the frenzied passion that came with my hand running through her hair. All I had to do was know how to play the role right: to hold the cups properly, speak eloquently, and carry myself with the assurance of a leading sitcom actor.

I handed Judith her glass.

"Cheers," I said.

"To what?" she asked.

"Furniture."

"Perfect," she said.

We raised our glasses to the air, and we toasted to furniture.

I sat down on the couch next to Judith. We both put our feet up on the coffee table, bending our knees so that we resembled a pair of children sitting bored and idle. She leaned over and rested her head on my shoulder. All of her exhaustion came through at that moment. Her head didn't land so much as it seemed to finally relent. She didn't say anything more and neither did I. I was still holding my glass in my hand, the ice slowly melting into the shallow pool of scotch whose scent occasionally wafted up and stung my nose, when I noticed that she had fallen asleep. It would have been too much to move, to nudge Judith's head even just an inch from its perch on my shoulder, which at that moment I believed to have been shaped with her head precisely in mind.

Approximately twenty-five minutes passed before Judith lifted her head on her own. I had counted each minute off on the clock hanging above the stove in the kitchen. Her mouth had hung slightly open the entire time, as if there had been something that she had been waiting to say but hadn't quite yet found the proper words for.

"I should get back home," she said when she opened her eyes. "I would hate to imagine what Naomi would do if she woke up and found that I wasn't there. Don't worry about walking me home or anything. I think I can get there safe."

"You really like that joke, don't you?"

"I don't have many to choose from."

She put one arm around my neck and pressed her cheek against mine. I didn't know what to do with my hands, so I left them dangling limp at my side for a second while Judith whispered into my ear, "Thank you for being so sweet." I gave in then and let my arms wrap, just barely, around her waist. All of the tenderness that I had stored inside of me came rushing to the surface of my skin. I bit down hard on my tongue to hold it back. I waited for her to lift her head toward mine, but it never happened.

She left immediately after that. I watched her from the top of the staircase as she made her way down to the street, and then followed her from my living-room window as she climbed the steps to her own house. We may not have been lovers, but that didn't stop me from thinking of her as such.

Naomi was back in my store the next day. I didn't ask her where she had been, or why she hadn't come by to see me all week. I told her simply, "You were missed," which she responded to with a shy smile.

She came in strapped with books that she hoisted onto the counter by standing on the tips of her toes. It was the first day of her Christmas break, and she had raided the local library for all it was worth. She opened the bag and pulled out the half-dozen books she had picked to make her way through the quiet winter weeks. Apparently, she had gone exclusively for size. *The Education of Henry Adams, Brewer's Dictionary of Phrase and Fable, The Brothers Karamazov, Plants and Animals of the Western Hemisphere,* and an *Atlas of the Modern World.*

"What do you plan on doing with all these books?"

"Reading them."

"Even the dictionary and atlas?"

She shook her head and rolled her eyes at me. She hadn't learned yet to conceal her scorn for my silly questions, and I know it sounds easy to say, but had she been able to explain her derision, I'm sure it would have had something to do with my adult impulse to place limits on her world.

"Seems like a lot for one girl to read. How long is your vacation?"

"Sixteen days, counting weekends."

"You better get started, then."

"What should we read first?"

It was that simple with her. She claimed me without even trying, while I, for my part, gratefully accepted her designation as one half of a "we" with nothing but pride.

"I don't know," I said. "You pick."

She laid the books next to one another on the counter, and then opened each one to a random page in the middle. She read out loud the history of the laurel tree in Greek mythology, a passage about the mountain lion in North America, and then the last pages of *The Brothers Karamazov*. Alyosha's speech to the young boys gathered around him, or perhaps it was the deliberately crude sketch drawing of the three brothers on the paper-back cover, won her over.

"This one," she said. "Let's read this one."

Inside the front flap of the book were the handwritten names of the dozen or so people who had checked the book out before Naomi. Instead of writing her name, Naomi had a thin paper receipt with the due date printed on it. She could never possess this book the way those other people had. It was one of those uselessly nostalgic and sentimental thoughts that serve only our own romantic ideals, but I couldn't help believing it was true nonetheless. I took a pencil out from behind the register and handed it to her.

"Write your name in here," I told her.

"You're not supposed to write in the books."

"I know. But this is different. This is just your name. And this way, anyone who picks up this book years and years from now will know that Naomi once read it."

I don't know if it was that idea or the opportunity to defy authority that appealed to her. Either way, she took the pencil and wrote her name carefully, in cursive, on the last slot available.

7

Lying on the grass on the edge of Dupont Circle, away from the shade cast by the office buildings and trees, I listen closely to the sirens. They don't fit in with the picturesque scene of office workers lunching on the grass, but there they are, faint, undoubtedly audible, and growing louder with each passing second. The couple that I followed to the circle from my store stand up and exit. As the sirens draw closer, the people lying on the grass look up from their books. Those who are strolling strain under the glare of the sun to see what's coming at them, while the people on the benches, comfortable and relaxed, try not to bother. There's more than one siren, perhaps as many as four or five, their sounds echoing and amplifying one another, so it's impossible to be certain. The sound quickly takes over the circle. No one has any option but to watch the parade of police motorcycles, cars, massive black SUVs, and black limos heading toward us. People begin to point in awe. Some pull out their cameras and take pictures, while others clasp their hands around their ears to block out the nearly deafening roar. A lasso of black cars forms around the circle, blowing past stoplights, oblivious to the motionless cars trapped in their lane and the people standing perfectly still at all the crosswalks. We all have the sense that someone of great import is passing, and that we are fulfilling our role as observers. It seems as if time has been temporarily suspended, the world placed on pause as we wait to return to our ordinary lives. In Ethiopia the story was similar. Troops used to line whatever route the emperor took hours in advance. They swept the streets clean of beggars, cripples, and trash, and had faithful loyalists stand on the side of the road, ready to bow as he passed. When the emperor was finally deposed at the start of the revolution, he was carried out of his palace in a blue Volkswagen Beetle. At the time I had thought of it as a silly and pointless thing to do, but now I can see how wrong I was. Few things are as important as the last impressions we make when leaving. Take away the whirling lights and blaring sirens of a motorcade and this is what you are left with: an old man, slightly senile, in the backseat of a beat-up car.

As the police cars vanish, I imagine an entirely empty motorcade whose sole purpose is to remind people what they are up against.

The clock at the bank on the corner flashes the time, 1:28, and the temperature, 72 degrees. Branches are swaying in the wind, shedding their petals, just like they're supposed to, while the red and yellow tulips along the perimeter of the circle bob their heads to the rhythm of the breeze. The lunch crowd is beginning to file back toward the offices and I stand up to join them. It's like watching the end of afternoon recess on a playground. We funnel into the circle's four exits, returning, no doubt out of habit, to the lessons of our childhood.

I walk to the pay phones near the metro entrance. I want to call my uncle Berhane to tell him that I'm getting on a train in the middle of the day to come see him. Over the course of the past two years, I have visited him three, maybe four times. We see each other almost exclusively in extreme circumstances. When his mother died in Ethiopia two years ago, we came together here in D.C. to mourn a woman whom, in the end, neither one of us really knew. We sat in his living room, our hands firmly clasped, in complete silence, as men and women whose names I hardly recognized entered the incense-filled room, offered their condolences, and sat quietly like black-draped ghosts on the paltry furniture. Tiny blue-and-white cups of coffee circulated ceaselessly around the room, along with plates of *injera* piled high with cabbage, greens, and chicken. A few women clicked their tongues in mourning as soon as they entered the apartment; I remember one man even wept. Everyone agreed it was God's will, and a powerful old priest from one of the Orthodox churches was even called up to confirm it. After three days, the guests stopped coming, and Berhane, two decades older than me with a soft, stoic face and sleepy eyes, told me gently that I could go back home now. Eight months later, his girlfriend's asylum application failed, and she moved to Canada to live with a cousin. On her last night in D.C., the three of us went to the nicest Ethiopian restaurant in the city and drank through the silence and awkwardness. This is the type of family we are. Two men who depend on each other in the oddest and most important circumstances. Even now, after nearly two decades in America, I continue to refer to him respectfully as Gashe.

I dial his number, and after a few rings, the answering machine picks up. I hear his soft, muted voice say, in its heavy accent, "Hello. Thank you for calling. You have reached the home of Berhane Selassie." It took him almost two years to remove my name from that recording. Every time I hear that greeting I feel a small pang of regret for having left him in that apartment alone. I don't have the heart to leave him a message and tell him I'm coming. It would only worry him, so instead I do what I do best. I close my eyes and hang up.

I call Joseph's restaurant next. He's been a waiter at the Colonial Grill for over eight years now, and I've never once been inside the restaurant to see him. The excuse I've offered has always been that I'm too busy with the store, but that doesn't hold any longer now, does it? When Joseph first began to work at the restaurant, he would demand that I come and eat there during his shift so he could, as he liked to say, "take care of me." "Come in sometime, Stephanos. Close the store. Take the day off. And I'll have you treated like the king of Ethiopia."

When I reminded him that the emperor had been killed and buried under a toilet, he shrugged his shoulders and said, "These things happen. We all make mistakes."

When the hostess answers, "Colonial Grill. How may I help you?" I ask her if Joseph Kahangi is working today. She hesitates for a moment and replies, "Yes, he is." Before she can ask who's calling, I hang up. Today is not a day for trivial questions or useless answers. I take another quarter and call my answering machine. I have two messages, both from Kenneth. He says the same thing in each one. "Pick up, Stephanos. Where are you?"

I take my last quarter and call Kenneth's office one more time. I want to tell him that today is a beautiful day, and not to worry. I want to reassure him and tell him that I am going to do something, with my store and with myself, just as he asked me to. I have one more name for him first: Valentine Strasser. It's an impossible name: Valentine Strasser. At twenty-five he became the youngest coup leader in Africa's history and the youngest head of state in the world. In pictures his small eyes peer out over a flat, hairless face too young to have killed and ruined so many lives. I hang up just after the first ring. Strasser, with his baby-soft criminal looks, is too fresh in our memories for this game.

I take the quarter back and call my store. I keep my finger on the lever. The phone rings once, twice, and then on the fourth ring, someone picks up. I'm too startled to speak, and so, apparently, is the person on the other end. Neither one of us says anything. It's been nearly two hours since I abandoned my store. Everything that has or has not happened to it since could fit into this silence.

I hear children yelling in the background. Their voices are happy, exuberant even. And why not? There is nothing in my store that they can't have. Someone shouts, "Get the fuck outta here," after which there is a tumbling, tossing noise. It's the sound of cans of soup raining on the ground, my store falling to pieces.

A steady but nervous voice, slightly frail, finally whispers, "Hello." It repeats itself, more confident and assured, a few seconds later. "Hello. Who is this?"

It's the "Who is this?" that gives it away. It's the same voice that in the morning yells out from the first-floor window, "Don't forget my milk," and in the evening, "You got my milk?" On the weekends the voice monitors my comings and goings, scrutinizes my clothes, tells me to polish my shoes, asks me whether or not I think it's going to rain, makes me pitchers of sweet iced tea, encourages me to come to church, and more recently, can sense my loneliness and occasional despair and tries to wash it away with a firm grip on my hand and a wet kiss on my cheek.

God bless you, Mrs. Davis, and all the widows of the world, I think as I hang up the phone.

☥

The escalators that lead down to the metro are vast and cavernous, an enormous yawning mouth that swallows and spits out thousands of people each day. My uncle lives at the end of the red train line in one of the poorer suburbs of Maryland. At worst, it's a twenty-minute ride on the metro and a half-hour walk from there, a paltry distance for two men who are otherwise thousands of miles away from any other living relative. There are no subdivisions, and you would be hard pressed to find even one well-manicured lawn. Instead of pleasant gated communities, twenty-story slabs of gray concrete apartment buildings line an overly congested road developed to the point of breaking with a dozen strip malls. In Ethiopia, my uncle barely ever figured into my family's life. A powerful, wealthy man, he lived just outside of Addis on a sprawling ranch that I visited only once as a child. It sat on the edge of a ridge with sweeping views of the shallow green valley below. It's difficult to remember that places like that ever existed. They seem conjured, the fictitious dreams of a hyperactive and lonely imagination. Today, all I can remember of the house are the dust-caked walls and the wooden rafter beams on the ceiling. I remember there were windows everywhere, and that entire rooms seemed to have been made of nothing but glass and light. The house, I learned later, was inspired by a picture of a Frank Lloyd Wright Prairie home my uncle had seen in an issue of *Architectural Digest*. Berhane designed the home himself, entirely from the memory of that photograph. The house, he said, was supposed to disappear into the landscape, invisible to the naked eye until just the last moment. Whatever his business was, he tended to it from there. He knew even then to be distrustful of the city.

His exact relationship to my mother remains a mystery. He is not her brother, but throughout my life, I have known him only as my uncle. He came to D.C. two years before me after having disappeared in the middle of the night without telling a single person. His house and all of his possessions, down to his car keys and family photographs, were left perfectly intact, as if he had disappeared into thin air just as his home had always suggested he would. Two weeks later troops showed up at his door, disgusted to find that the entire estate had become occupied by the relatives of his maid, guard, and cook. The servants who lived on his estate never knew where he was going, and for this they were beaten (but never killed) by the roaming gangs that spent their evenings knocking on the doors of the rich. No one tended to the house, and each man and woman lived briefly in a state of garish splendor, consuming food and clothes with the full knowledge that none of it would last.

The red-line train bound for the suburbs of Maryland is delayed. The trains of this city continue to amaze me, regardless of how long I live here. It's not just their size, but their order, the sense you get when riding them that a higher, regulatory power is in firm control, even if you yourself are not. All around me people check their watches, shake their heads, and stamp their feet. The platform begins to fill up as people instinctively begin to cluster around the gleaming fluorescent-lit billboards. Behind me is an ad for the Virginia community college I briefly attended. The school's ad campaign and motto, "Taking You to Where You Want to Be," is splayed across the bottom in gold-faced letters tilting as if caught in a breeze. Four students—one white, one black, one Asian, one Hispanic—are walking across the lawn, books in arm, smiling at one another. After seventeen years here, I am certain of at least one thing: the liberal idea of America is at its best in advertising. Sixteen years ago, I saw those same smiling faces strolling across the neatly trimmed lawn on a roadside billboard, a pastoral scene that at the time was so appealing to me I was willing to buy it with no questions asked. In the absence of a family, a home, friends, and a country, being a student was as complete an identity as I had ever hoped for. There was a power to the word, something akin to being the citizen of a wealthy, foreign country. To the friends and acquaintances of my uncle, all refugees like him, I was already a moderate success, someone to be teased and bragged about over dinner conversations. To my mother in Ethiopia, I was the penultimate accomplishment of a long-awaited dream. The first aim of the refugee is to survive, and having done that, that initial goal is quickly replaced by the general ambitions of life. I didn't leave Ethiopia to attend classes in the northern suburbs of Virginia, but to hear the story told then, that was what I had done. During my one year in college, I brandished my title as frequently as possible. I introduced myself as a student to every person I met, often without their asking. I made it the raison d'être for my being in America, even as the famine in Ethiopia briefly dominated the news, along with hints at the long-standing civil war in the north. Images of starving children with bloated bellies and fly-covered faces were ubiquitous. When pressed for a response, all I could do was shake my head and agree that yes, what was happening in Ethiopia was indeed a tragedy. But what did I know about any of this? I was a student, studying engineering. All I wanted was to tuck my books under my arm and stroll across the campus lawn with that permanent grin stretched across my face.

By the time the train pulls into the station, the platform is thick with people pressed tightly together. We all squeeze our way into the train, avoiding eye contact even though we can feel the breath of the person next to us blowing on our neck. Standing next to me is an exceptionally tan young blond woman with a ponytail sticking out of her baseball cap. She's wearing a blue Georgetown tank top, gray Georgetown shorts, and a black backpack with the Georgetown insignia stitched into the center. I always note the fresh, scrubbed faces of the city's collegiate crowd with a smatter of envy and wonder. Joseph, in particular, has taught me to appreciate them. He still makes frequent trips to the Georgetown campus, using his long-expired student ID to get him into the library, where he will pull a half-dozen books off the shelves and pile them haphazardly around a table. He likes to play the role of an aspiring academic lost in his deep thoughts about poetry, religion, and politics. The handful of adult continuing-education classes he took there scarred him forever. He used all of his savings to pay for noncredit courses in American Religious Pluralism, Symbolism in Dante's *Commedia*, and Gender Relations in Twentieth-Century Post-Colonial Africa. Almost five years have passed since then, a mere technicality for Joseph, who continues even now to reread his class notes and highlight passages from the *Inferno*.

Through a round aperture I saw appear,
Some of the beautiful things that Heaven bears,

Where we came forth, and once more saw the stars.

When he's drunk, he likes to declare those to be the most perfect lines of poetry ever written. "Think about it," he says.

"Dante is finally coming out of hell, and that is what he sees. 'Some of the beautiful things that heaven bears.' It's perfect, I tell you. Simply perfect. I told my teacher that no one can understand that line like an African because that is what we lived through. Hell every day with only glimpses of heaven in between."

There was hardly a single thing in Joseph's life, though, that hadn't become a metaphor for Africa. From great lines of poetry to the angle of falling light on a spring afternoon, he saw flashes of the continent wherever he went. Kenneth hated him for this.

"If you miss it so much," he yelled at him once, "why don't you go back? Then you don't have to say every day, 'This is like Africa, that is like Africa.' You can't go back, though. You would rather miss it comfortably from here instead of hating it every day from there."

Joseph had no response. For once, his symbolic grandiloquence was too big even for him. The words "That is what it's like to be an African" always hovered around the edge of every conversation Joseph had. At times, it was almost miraculous the way he would manage to find a way to insert them. There wasn't a sport played in the world that couldn't be better grasped by the African mind. And as for politics, who understood its weight, capriciousness, and value better than the citizens of a continent devastated by coups and tyrannical old men? A history teacher at my northern Virginia community college said once that there had been only three real revolutions in the past two hundred years: the French, Chinese, and Russian. Everything else was merely a rebellion, insurrection, uprising, protest, strike. Tsk. He didn't know how easily an entire society could be made and remade. More than just having garish billboards painted on the sides of buildings and multiple-story statues in city squares,

Africa's dictators were busy reshaping their countries to their own liking.

It takes the train less than fifteen minutes to leave the city limits. That's the dirty secret about D.C. For all of its stature and statues, the city could just as easily have been one of the grander suburbs of America, an appendix hooked to Virginia or Maryland. As the joke goes, everyone who has lived here long enough suffers from an inevitable inferiority complex, size not being the least of it. When the train rushes above ground, we've already crossed into the outskirts of the city. The buildings, old brick factories and warehouses, are all marked with the familiar bright red and yellow bubble letters of Disco Dan. The name is everywhere, tagged onto the side of the tracks, buildings, and rusted water towers. A running billboard competing with the ads for Schlitz malt liquor and used-car lots. Disco Dan—offering nothing but himself and his vanity—has them all beat. For as long as I've lived in the city, he has been with me. It's more than just gratitude that rises up involuntarily when I see his name spread across an abandoned brown factory lot, under the broken windows, layered in multiple colors of red, yellow, blue, and white, each character so monstrously large and bright that all you see for a second is the name. I remember another aphorism of my father's, one that he used to say whenever we passed someone pissing openly in the street: add color to life when you can.

8

I spent the next three days, after she picked it out, reading *The Brothers Karamazov* with Naomi. With school closed for the holidays, she came to the store every day just shortly after waking up. Her mother would bundle her in way too many clothes for the short walk from their house to the store so that the first thing Naomi had to do when she came in was peel off the layers of clothing, which seemed designed to insulate her from the neighborhood as much as from the cold. I kept the stool waiting for her behind the counter so that when she came in she knew without asking where to sit. She piled her coat, gloves, sweater, hat, and scarf into a corner next to the register and then pulled her library copy off the counter where she had left it the day before.

On our first morning together Naomi demanded that I be the one who read first. She laid the book on the counter and said, "Here, you start."

"Shouldn't you be the one to start?" I asked her.

"That's not the way it works," she said. "First you and then me."

I read forty or fifty pages that first day. Naomi read none. After I read the first page I waited for her to pick up where I had left off, but she insisted, in a voice that bordered on pleading, that I continue.

"One more," she said at first. And when that page had been completed, she added another "one more" to that, until eventually there were so many "pleases" and "pretty pleases" and "come on, pleases" that I was left utterly defenseless.

I looked up every couple of pages to see if Naomi was still paying attention, and of course she was. Her attention, in fact, never seemed to waver. I felt her staring at me sometimes when my eyes were focused on the page, and I realized she was taking it all in, not just the words, but me, and the scene that we had created together. Here we were, an older man and a girl young enough to be the man's daughter, sitting in a store on a winter morning reading a novel together. I tried not to notice too much, to simply just live, but that was impossible. Every time I looked at her I became aware of just how seemingly perfect this time was. I thought about how years from now I would remember this with a crushing, heartbreaking nostalgia, because of course I knew even then that I would eventually find myself standing here alone. And just as that knowledge would threaten to destroy the scene, Naomi would do something small, like turn the page too early or shift in her chair, and I would be happy once again.

I had more customers then, and I treated each interruption to our reading as an assault on my privacy. When someone I didn't know entered the store, Naomi would mark where I had left off so that I could keep my eyes on the person wandering around the aisles. She would take the book out of my hand, put her finger on the exact word or sentence I had just concluded, and hold it there until I returned. I kept one man, who came to the counter with a single roll of toilet paper under his arm, waiting for more than a minute while I finished reading a page I had just started. At first he smiled and was charmed by what he saw. He was one of the new white faces in the neighborhood who bought all of my bottled water. The charm wore off when I refused to acknowledge him. He responded by slamming the roll on the counter, inches away from my face, and storming out. Naomi and I read on.

I slipped into the characters as I read. I grumbled and bellowed, slammed my fist onto the counter, and threw my arms wide open. I knew this was exactly what my father would have done had he been the one reading. He would have made the story an event, as grand and real as life. He must have told me hundreds, perhaps even thousands, of stories, not just at night, but throughout the course of any given day, over breakfast, during lunch, in the middle of a conversation he might have been carrying on with my mother or friends. There was no wrong time with him, or if there was, he didn't live long enough for me to see it.

The stories he invented himself he told with particular delight. They all began the same way, with the same lighthearted tone, with a small wave of the hand, as if the world were being brushed to the side, which I suppose for him it actually was.

"Ah, that reminds me. Did I tell you about—
The shepherd who beat his sheep too hard
The farmer who was too lazy to plow his fields
The hyena who laughed himself to death
The lion who tried to steal the monkey's dinner
The monkey who tried to steal the lion's dinner?"
If I had heard the story before, I let him tell it to me again. His

performance was that good, his love of a story that obvious. Henry the chauffeur and his lavish monkey employers had their predecessors here, even though I never told Naomi that part of the story. Instead, when Fyodor Karamazov spoke, I waved my hands wildly in the air. I grumbled in a deep baritone and tried as hard as I could to do my father proud.

"Ah, you fools," I shouted out, and Naomi smiled in delight.

Naomi found each of the characters as real as anyone she met in the street.

"Oooh, I hate him," she would cry out after a particularly cruel antic on the part of the elder Karamazov. "He's such a mo-ron." When it came to Alyosha, though, the youngest and gentlest of the Karamazov brothers, she was willing to fall completely in love. I read his scenes and lines with all of the aplomb and grace I could gather. Sometimes while I read, Naomi would lay her head against my arm or in my lap and rest there, wide awake and attentive, until forced to move. It was just enough to make me see how one could want so much more out of life.

The customers who came to the store regularly took to Naomi immediately. She judged them harshly, as I knew she would. The five to eight drunk old men who made their way into the store every afternoon to pick up another bottle of malt liquor were never rewarded with so much as a hello despite their best efforts. "Who's that pretty young thang you got working be-hind the counter now, Stephanos? I know she can't be related to you, not with a face as pretty as that." "What's your name, pretty girl? I used to have a daughter that looked just like you. She had the same pretty eyes that you do."

Naomi met all of their attention, sincere and good-natured as it may have been, with a fake grin that they took to be a mark of shyness. I knew better. Once, as one of the men was walking out of the store, I saw her roll her eyes and heard her whisper, "Take a bath." The man, whom I knew only as Mr. Clark, paused just slightly at the door when she said that. Like all of the other men, he was old enough to have been her father or grandfather. He wore thick glasses taped together in the center, and the same pair of rumpled brown pants that hit his ankles just an inch too high. His hair had gone mostly gray, and on warmer days he passed his afternoons sleeping on one of the benches surrounding General Logan. I didn't know him to be a good, or bad, man. I knew only that every day he chose to lose himself in as many bottles of alcohol as he could afford rather than waste his energy facing his life head on. When he turned his head toward her, there was a resigned sadness to his expression that neither Naomi nor I could bear to look at. His face seemed to say that if given half a chance, he would have done anything not to be judged by this eleven-year-old girl who wore pink cashmere.

When we finished reading just after lunch, Naomi refused to go back home. Rather than leave the store she asked, "So what do we do now?"

It was easy enough to invent small tasks to keep her with me. On the first day of her vacation I gave her a broom that she pushed up and down the aisles. She was meticulous. She swept each piece of tile once, and then twice, as if she were brushing an ancient artifact free of centuries of dust and sand. She swept the floor underneath the lowest shelves, which had rarely seen the bristles of a broom.

"This place is filthy," Naomi said. And while I may have been hurt just slightly by her judgment, I also wanted to make it better for her so I could be rewarded with a hundred mornings and afternoons just like this one.

Judith came as usual to pick Naomi up at five or a few minutes before. On that first day, Naomi saw her mother just before she came in. At the last second, she picked up her copy of *The Brothers Karamazov* and in that same insistent voice of hers said, "Come on, Mr. Stephanos, one more chapter." I saw Judith walking across the street, just steps away. I grabbed the book from Naomi's hands and turned to a random page near the beginning.

"Fyodor Karamazov," I continued without looking up as Judith entered the store. She paused just inside the door, while Naomi leaned over the counter with one hand resting on her chin as if she were reading the pages with me. When I looked up I saw Naomi trying as hard as she could to act as if she were listening. We had become accomplices.

"So," Judith said after a few seconds of standing in the doorway and watching us pretend to read. "I see she even has you reading to her now." She had her arms folded over her chest and was leaning slightly against the wall. She hadn't caught on to the act we were putting on, but she wasn't completely fooled, either.

I closed the book and acted as if I were noticing her for the first time.

"We've been taking turns," I said.

"Is that true, Naomi?"

Naomi nodded her head vigorously.

"Pull up a chair and join us," I offered.

"Depends on what you're reading."

I showed Judith the cover of the book.

"A little dense, isn't it?"

"I didn't pick it out. Naomi did."

"Of course she did. How else could she keep you reading to her for hours?"

I wanted to applaud Naomi for her foresight. Judith and I

were both being conned, but neither of us particularly minded. To earn that kind of trust and affection from a child is to find out that you may have just been a better person than you believed all along.

"So is that why we're reading this?" I asked Naomi.

She did what few children could have done. She looked me directly in the eye and said, "Yes."

"We have to go now, though," Judith said. "It's getting late and we have dinner plans."

"One more chapter," Naomi pleaded.

"Tomorrow," Judith said. "Tomorrow you can stay as long as you like."

Tomorrow did not come fast enough, but when it finally did arrive after a restless night, I was ready. I had called Joseph as soon as I returned home so I could explain everything that had happened to him.

"Tell me again now, what did she say when she left the store?" he asked me.

"She said, 'You can stay as long as you like.'"

There was a long stretch of silence on Joseph's end as he deliberated over the meaning of Judith's words.

"What else did she say?" he asked.

"That was it."

"Was she smiling at you?"

"No. She may have, and I just missed it."

I could almost see Joseph shaking his head on the other end of the phone. He breathed in deeply and sighed loudly enough for me to hear him.

"What do you know about this woman?" he asked me.

"What do you mean?" I said. "I know plenty."

"Don't get mad at me, Stephanos. I'm just asking you simple

questions. Relationships with women are tricky. Trust me. I know about these things. You've never dated an American before."

Joseph was kind enough not to remind me that since coming to America I had never had a relationship of any kind beyond brief one-night encounters.

"American women are different," he continued. "Remember that. You never know what's in their hearts."

He was talking like a scorned lover. I thought of him in his restaurant, as the Rouge that he had known years earlier in a different life sat at a table with a crowd of people eating, laughing, while he sat hiding in the back.

"Don't worry," I told him. "I'll be fine. I know what I'm doing."

After we hung up the phone I went back to my bathroom mirror. I stared hard and long at my reflection. I ran my hands through my hair and turned my head from one side to the other. I was determined to find something that someone like Judith could describe as beautiful. It seemed entirely possible if I turned my head the right way, smiled the proper smile, and made sure the light hit my face at the correct angle. I lifted up my chin and turned my head a few degrees to the left. I smiled with only the right side of my face. I washed my face, dried it, and then washed it again. With each blink a new face looked back at me, simultaneously handsome and grotesque and nondescript. Who was I? That was all I wanted to know.

The following morning I read three chapters to Naomi. Afterward we rearranged all the items on the shelves. We threw away the cans of expired food buried in the back, brushed the dust off the boxes of cereal, and chipped away at the ice in the freezer. After two days of her being there, the store looked better than it had in years. The aisles were clean; each item faced in the proper direction. I swept the old condom and candy wrappers that littered the ground in front of the store and in the alley. I added a touch of white paint to the northwest corner of the store, where the paint had peeled back in long thin strips to reveal an even older coat of faded lime green paint. I tightened the screws on the shelves that had begun to sag from neglect. I even replaced the fluorescent light bulbs that had long since begun to dim. They had given the store a muted, faded look that I had thought of as somehow fitting, but now, with Naomi in the store, I felt eager, even anxious to make it a place that I wasn't afraid to look at. At the end of the afternoon, when I stopped and looked back on all that we had done, I felt the pride of ownership that Americans always speak of with such reverence.

At four I started to count down the minutes until Judith arrived. I wanted her to see what I had done with the store, to marvel in approval, to see the hidden potential behind the shabby exterior.

At four-twenty I began to ask Naomi questions.

"How is your mother doing?"

"Fine."

"Do you have any dinner plans tonight?"

"I don't know."

"Did she say anything to you about it?"

"I don't think so."

"Can you remember her saying she had anywhere to go tonight?"

"No."

"Think," I said. "Did she say anything at all?"

I felt the desperation in my voice and backed down at the last second. Naomi eyed me suspiciously. I paid her back with a candy bar that she hid in the inside pocket of her coat.

When Judith finally arrived, prompt as usual at five minutes before five, she came bearing tea and hot chocolate. She carried them over in two metal thermoses that came with spill-proof lids and ergonomically curved chrome handles. In her purse, she carried teacups and a little jar of honey. She opened the door with a "Surprise," and then quickly went to work setting out the cups and drinks on the counter.

"What's the occasion?" I asked her.

"No occasion," she said. "But I figured if we were going to read, there was no reason why we couldn't do it properly."

I noted the "we" in her last sentence. I held on to it and told myself that I would use it against Joseph later. "We were going to read," I would tell him. We.

Judith poured tea for the two of us, and a cup of hot chocolate for Naomi.

"I figured you had milk and sugar in the store," she said. "But I can't ever remembering seeing any honey."

She was right. I didn't carry any honey. I had sold the last bottle of it three, maybe four years ago and never thought of ordering any more.

The three of us sipped our tea and hot chocolate just as the sun was setting for the day. The first of the evening commuters were beginning to rush past the store on their way home, traffic was building up along the circle and on Massachusetts Avenue, and the temperature was a moderate 36 degrees, just cool enough to lend a certain urgency to returning home at the end of the day. We had managed to avoid all of that, like three prisoners locked in a comfortable cell that afforded them a view of a world they no longer cared to join. I remember looking out the window of the store and watching men and women walk briskly with their coats and scarves wrapped around their necks and feeling a certain pity for them.

Business always thinned out shortly after six, when the last of the rush-hour commuters finally made their way home. Rather than try to read through the interruptions, Judith and Naomi simply waited for me around the counter while I tended to the last customers of the day. The two of them sat on opposing silver stools salvaged from the garbage. They even held their cups delicately the same way: with one finger looped around the handle and the other hand used to support the base and side. From the back I watched Naomi as she timed her sips to match her mother's.

At half-past six I quietly turned the sign to "Closed" without dimming any of the lights or locking the door. I took my place behind the counter. Judith suggested that we take turns reading.

"You read one page," she said. "And then I'll read the next."

"And what about Naomi?"

"She can pretend she's still paying attention."

We read back and forth for half an hour that night, until all the tea had been drunk and Naomi had taken to swirling her finger in the bottom of her cup. For those thirty minutes I had it all, and perhaps if I had been a wiser man I would have been content with just that.

9

By the time the train pulls into the Silver Spring station, I am one of only four people left in the car. We're spread out evenly between the rear and the front, as if we have chosen sides in some childish debate and are refusing to meet in the middle. I wish empty trains inspired more recklessness in the people forced to share them. There's a solitude and isolation that come with knowing that out of everyone you had begun your journey with, only you and the few faces across the aisle are left. That alone seems enough to make a connection, but as it stands, the opposite is always true. The empty space, whether it's only a few feet or the entire car, becomes impassable. Perhaps it's the embarrassment of being alone, the fear of being exposed, and the risk of losing one's anonymity that make us shy away from one another precisely when we should feel emboldened. I can't even bring myself to look at the woman facing me from the other end of the car. That's how naked a nearly empty train can make me feel.

It's still the middle of the day, and despite the growing heat I've decided to walk to my uncle's apartment. The walk to the apartment complex is a hostile one. The sidewalk narrows to a silver streak of cracked concrete that runs adjacent to a four-lane road densely populated with extended city buses and a continuous stream of cars. I always feel like a sad, pathetic creature while walking along this road. The world seems entirely unfit to handle my skinny, long-legged body, and the curious, often hostile glares of the drivers in their cars confirm it. Today, though, I've decided to seek pleasure wherever I can, which means finding comfort in the exhaust-choked air, and in the strain I feel while struggling up the steep incline that leads to the Silver Rock complex where my uncle lives.

I can imagine his surprise and gratitude at my unexpected visit. He will want to make tea for the both of us. He will insist on feeding me whatever he has in his refrigerator, even though he won't have anything to offer besides leftovers from whatever Ethiopian restaurant he ate at the night before. Before I can tell him anything about my life, he will want to hear everything he can about my mother and brother. He will want the details of their health and about my brother's plans for the future now that he has graduated college. When I tell him that they are both doing well, he will kiss the air and thank God, at least twice, for His grace. I know that he will reprimand me gently, and with good humor, for not having visited him sooner. He will shake his head, rub his hand across his nearly bald head, and then blame himself for being guilty of the same crime. When he speaks, he will do so slowly and deliberately, carefully choosing each word because he is nothing if not an exceptionally thoughtful man. I will assure him that the absence is entirely my fault; that I've been distracted with work, which is still going okay (another kiss to the air and a single "thank God"). Regardless of what I say, he will stomp one foot firmly on the ground and in the end insist that no, I am his responsibility, and therefore I can claim none of the guilt for my own. Ever since I dropped out of school, he has tried hard to hide his disappointment. He worries about my future, and yet he's always played a part in reassuring my mother about the quality and state of my life. When he asks me about the store, I will tell him that I have plans for selling it. Or I will tell him I've already looked into selling it. Or that I already have someone interested in taking it off my hands. Anything to reassure him.

I'm covered in sweat when I reach the apartment complex. I catch my reflection in the building's door. Sweat is streaming down the side of my face. I look exactly like what I am: a desperate man, on the verge of middle age, with only the money in his pocket to spare. I have dark rings under my eyes, a nose and forehead damp with sweat. My shirt collar has an old coffee stain on it, and the sides of my pant pockets have a streak of dirt running down the side. I take a second to tuck in my shirt, pat down the edges of my hair, and wipe the sweat off my brow with the edges of my sleeve. I pray that I don't run into anyone I know.

There are twenty-eight floors to the building, and of those twenty-eight floors, at least twenty-six are occupied exclusively by other Ethiopians who, like my uncle, moved here sometime after the revolution and found to their surprise that they would never leave. Within this building there is an entire world made up of old lives and relationships transported perfectly intact from

Ethiopia. To call the building insular is to miss the point entirely. Living here is as close to living back home as one can get, which is precisely why I moved out after two years and precisely why my uncle has never left. Hardly a word of English is spoken inside of these doors. The hallways on every floor smell of *wat*, coffee, and incense. The older women still travel from apartment to apartment dressed in slippers and white blankets that they keep wrapped around their heads, just as if they were still walking through the crowded streets of Addis. The children keep only the friendships sanctioned by their parents. There are a few families who occupy entire floors. They run them like minor villages with children, grandchildren, grandparents, and in-laws all living within shouting distance of one another. There is a beauty and a terror to those floors. Only once did I ever step onto one of them and see it firsthand. When I got off the elevator, I was met by a row of open apartment doors, each one guarded by a young woman who stepped into the doorway and stared at me with more apprehension and fear than I've ever been greeted by. I turned back to the elevator immediately, feeling as if I had intruded onto something sacred, something that I had no right to witness or speak of again.

My uncle stands out from the rest of the building. That he is only one man, with no wife, mother, or children, gives him an independence and peculiarity that no one here is comfortable with. He is respected because of the money and power he once had in Ethiopia, because his name was once associated with the cabinet members and princes of the old empire. He is also mocked now by some for exactly the same reason. Berhane Selassie. It's a beautiful name. Translated into English, it means Light of the Holy Trinity. He no longer has his money or his prestige, but he has his reserve, and his corner apartment on the twenty-fourth floor. For Silver Rock, it's a beautiful apartment. I believe he took as much time preparing its rooms as he did studying the design for the house he built for himself. It no more fits in with the dilapidated exterior—the dimly lit hallways, crumbling paint, and broken elevators—than he does.

Only one of the elevators is working today. A line builds up in front of it, forcing a round of general greetings with people whose faces, much less names, I can hardly recall. I know that there's a curiosity surrounding me. There's an upturned glance behind every *salaam* and *tadias* that I exchange. I'm being measured for everything. For my clothes, hair, shoes, for my readiness to offer a proper greeting and good-bye. Sometimes I think of my decision to leave this building as an escape, while at other times it seems more like an abandonment. I try not to take the thought too seriously, but when every eye you catch seems to hold an accusation or question behind it, a decision has to be made. Either I left to create a new life of my own, one free from the restraints and limits of culture, or I turned my back on everything I was and that had made me. Each familiar face waiting for the elevator seems to want to ask the same questions: What have you done with yourself, where have you gone, and who do you think you are? I know there would be a fair amount of pleasure behind the pity that would greet me if my life were ever laid bare before this crowd.

I'm pressed into the back of the elevator with at least fifteen other people. There's a joke waiting to be had here. How many Ethiopians can you fit into an elevator? All of them. What do you call an elevator full of Ethiopians? An oxymoron. Once the elevator begins to move, the gossip begins. It's disguised as innocent conversation between two women. Speaking much louder than necessary, one woman claims to have seen Dr. Negatu's daughter getting out of a cab by herself at sunrise. To make matters worse, she was sitting in the front seat. The news is followed by the customary tsking of sound judgment being passed. It's soon followed up with the other news of the day. Those who don't join in on the conversation simply stand quietly like myself, complicit and greedy. In one protracted elevator ride there are rumors of infidelity, abuse, drugs, unemployment. It all amounts to one thing: proof of a vanishing culture. Time, distance, and nostalgia have convinced these women that back in Ethiopia, we were all moral and perfect, all of which is easier to believe when you consider the lives that most of us live now. With our menial jobs and cramped apartments, it's impossible not to want to look back sometimes and pretend there was once a better world, one where husbands were faithful, children were obedient, and life was easy and wonderful.

With enough time, one woman says in Amharic, there won't be any Ethiopians. They'll all become American.

I can't help but smile whenever I hear that line. By even the most liberal standards, I would easily stand convicted of the same crime. I can count the number of Ethiopian friends still in my life with two fingers. I go out of my way to avoid the restaurants and bars frequented by other Ethiopians of my generation. My phone calls home are infrequent. I eat *injera* only on social occasions. I consider the old emperor to have been a tyrant, not a god. When I try to pray, it's only to ask God to forgive me for not believing in Him in the first place. And of course there had been Judith and Naomi, who alone could have set every gossiping tongue on fire for months.

I still have keys to Berhane's apartment, but I'm reluctant to use them right away. It's been too long since I've lived here, and I can't help but feel like a stranger every time I enter this apartment. I knock nearly a dozen times before accepting the fact that he's not home. Only then do I let myself in.

My uncle's apartment hasn't changed in the slightest detail since I moved out. I'm grateful to him for this small measure of consistency. He's kept all of the furniture exactly the same, even though he's been talking of buying a new couch or dining-room table for years. He's attached to the old ones. He can't help but be. I'm not sure what else in the world he has to believe in if not the couch and table that have stayed with him for the past nineteen years. That's the same couch I slept on, the same one I made every night and unmade every morning before dressing up to begin my day as a student or bellhop. At night, I slept on that couch and relived old fantasies and memories. I thought of my father. I remembered the way he cried at funerals, baptisms, and weddings, how any form of joy or pain seemed to always be too much for him to bear. I remembered him, a tall, slight, discerning man, in his suits and ties and in the long-gaited walk that I struggled to keep pace with. I saw the corpses that lay rotting on unpaved dusty roads with the words "traitor" or "Communist" written in blood on the chest, and the furious mobs that roamed the streets at night. I saw my father's face just before three soldiers in tattered uniforms escorted him out of our house. I never saw what death did to his face, whether or not it aged it, or perhaps even restored it to some long-vanished peaceful state. I did imagine it involuntarily while lying awake and staring across the living room to the glass doors that lead out to the balcony I sometimes imagined leaping off. In my mind, his face was untouched, free from any bruises or scars the soldiers might have left, his eyes, nose, and mouth impossibly perfect. I gave him a wonderful funeral, complete with all of the rites the dead deserve: a body, casket, and flowers, along with a priest and a cast of mourners who followed him all the way to his family's burial ground just outside of Addis. All of that happened on that couch.

I take a seat on the couch, slide off my shoes, and rest my tired feet on the coffee table. I'm not surprised to find that the springs have all held up, and that even the cushions are hardly any worse for wear. Preservation comes naturally to my uncle. It's part of what made him so diligent and devoted a caretaker to me. When I came home from school or work in the evenings, I often found him sitting on the recliner facing the couch, mending a pair of my socks or removing the stains from one of the two white shirts I had to wear as part of my work uniform. He could have easily been someone's grandmother with the way he rocked silently in that chair tending to the needs of his nephew. We barely spoke during the few hours we managed to share with each other every evening. Nothing more than a few tender kisses on the cheek followed by some generally insignificant statement about classes and work. He never tolerated any diversion into his own life. In the mornings he worked as a cabdriver and in the evenings he worked as a parking attendant at the Capitol Hotel. His life was determined by cars, tips, and making change. For a man who before coming to America had rarely ever driven his own car, the role reversal was always noted with his customary irony. "Perhaps," he would say, "if I went back to Ethiopia I could get a job driving the general now living in my house. Although I would kill the both of us on our first trip out." Any questions I may have had for him about his day or his fares were always met with a stern grin and a reminder that a man his age didn't have to answer any questions from a man of mine. On particularly good days, though, he would come home grinning and when pressed for a reason, he would respond enthusiastically, "Gas is so cheap!"

His mouth stretches to the limits of his face whenever he repeats that line, and in his eyes you can still see remnants of the humorous, snobbish young man he had once been. He still drives his cab, but not as frequently. The car and the license to operate it are entirely his now. What he makes from his fares he splits into two: one half is tucked away into a silver lockbox, the other half is wired back to Ethiopia at the end of every month. There was never much money in this apartment. Between the two of us we made just enough to cover our bills and pay my school fees. Like anyone who is poor, we each learned to find some small pleasures wherever we could. In the summertime we slept on the floor with the balcony doors pulled wide open. We slept with one thin blanket and a small fan that blew down on us from the coffee table. I remember those nights as being the best nights of sleep I had in that apartment. They were dreamless nights, free of memories, and I was grateful for that. My uncle said once that he often thought of his time in Sudan when he lay sleeping on the floor next to me. "The only difference," he said, "was that there were ten to fifteen of us sleeping on the floor together. We had pooled our money to pay for one room away from the refugee camp. The room wasn't any bigger than this one. The floor was made of dirt and clay that kept it cool at night. I remember trying to lift my nose above the feet in front of me to smell the wind." Before reaching Sudan, he had spent nearly a month walking through the countryside at night. He slept in the bush during the day and walked constantly through the evening. Half of the group of people he had met along the way perished somewhere in the desert, their bodies prayed over briefly before being left behind as carrion. He remembers those scorched summer nights spent pressed against the ground and someone's feet as the best nights of sleep he has ever had.

The silver lockbox where he keeps his money hidden is in his bedroom closet behind a stack of cardboard boxes full of letters and newspaper clippings that he's been saving for years. For as long as he has been living in the United States, he's been writing letters to the government. Every cabinet secretary from education to the interior has received a letter, along with the National Security Agency, the Congressional Budget Office, the various speakers of the House along with the Senate minority and majority leaders, the chairs of every major congressional committee, the White House chiefs of staff, the heads of the Republican and Democratic National Committees, and every senator or congressperson who has ever sponsored a bill he was even remotely interested in. The letters were all neatly typed and printed out in duplicates on his Brother electronic typewriter. Each response he's received he has stapled to his own letter and filed away. Taken all together, they form a running dialogue between one man, himself, and an indifferent, if not wholly silent, partner.

One of those boxes contains only the letters he has written to the presidents of the United States. Those letters, unlike any of the others, are personal, although they grow increasingly distant with time. The ones written in the past five years are simply the letters of a concerned and active citizen (Berhane is not, in fact, a citizen—only a permanent resident, which he will remain until he dies, because in his heart, he will always be in Ethiopia). In tone and in content, they are no different from any of the other letters concerning policy that he has written to other government officials, great and small alike.

These early letters to Presidents Carter and Reagan are my favorite items in this apartment. If he were to die tomorrow, they would be the only things of his that I would want to keep. My uncle doesn't even know that I'm aware of their existence. He has them stored at the bottom of his closet in a blue-and-white box, unmarked, out of embarrassment or pride, I'm not quite sure which. When I lived with him I read through them every day while he was at work. I memorized passages and then later puzzled over the man who had written them. They were unlike any other part of his personality: open, emotive, and free. They are deeply personal, but they are not crazy. Like any letter, they are a plea to be heard. I'm not sure who else my uncle could have spoken to about such things when he first came here. There was no one who could bear to hear his story about what he had lost and suffered. He was surrounded by other war-torn refugees, none of whom had achieved any measure of peace with their own past.

His first letter was to President Carter. Despite the effort it takes to find it, I search through the box, skimming past the letters he wrote to Reagan in his second term (frustrated and disappointed), and the ones written during his first (desperately optimistic). The letter is near the middle of the stack. He hasn't forgotten about it any more than I have.

Dear President Carter,

I am writing to you as a recent immigrant to the United States. I have come here from Ethiopia, where I'm sure you know there is currently a bloody war happening. I am one of those people for whom nothing is left of their home country. Everything I have has been taken away from me. For many ages, the United States and Ethiopia have been close allies. There is a deep friendship between our two countries. Therefore, it is imperative that the United States, along with

Ethiopia's friends in Europe, come to her aid at this critical juncture in her history. I am confident that with U.S. assistance, Ethiopia will be able to return to her former state immediately.

I think it's the naïveté of that letter that keeps us returning to it. I've never seen my uncle's expression while he reads it, but I imagine that there's at least a faint smile spread across his face. I think he would be amused, as I am now, at that sentence, "There is a deep friendship between our two countries." The sentiment is somewhere between schoolyard logic and the type of alliances you see only in movies that take place in galaxies far, far away. The awkward sentence, the one that is still difficult to read, happens near the very beginning: "I am one of those people for whom nothing is left of their home country." You can hear the syntax twist and strain as the sentence tries to make clear, without revealing too much, its full intention. I love the opening of that sentence, "I am one of those people . . ." From that point, the sentence could have gone in an infinite number of directions. I am one of those people who always cry at weddings. I am one of those people who's always late for meetings. I am one of those people who always look good in red. Losing a country seems like such a casual and mundane affair when introduced that way.

My uncle is a quick learner. Soon, he shed his innocence. He learned to write sentences that were sparer and more detailed. He clipped articles out of the *New York Times* and *Washington Post* and included them with his letters.

Dear President Carter,
You may have read yesterday's New York Times *article on the current crisis in Ethiopia. The newspaper says that there*

are widespread reports of arrests and disappearances throughout the country. I want to tell you personally that these disappearances are in fact executions. This month alone I have learned of the death of at least ten friends of mine. There are many more, I am sure, that I have yet to learn about. Those that died were all taken from their homes, in front of their wives and children. My brother-in-law, Shibrew Stephanos, was one of those men. He was beaten in front of his wife and two sons by government troops and then carried out of the house. The soldiers who arrested him said he was an anti-revolutionary because they had found some flyers in his office. Shibrew Stephanos was a good man and an excellent father. I implore you not to let his death, and the death of so many others like him, pass in vain.

He was wrong on two counts in that letter. My father was not carried out of the house. He walked out on his own. He was insistent on that point. It was the one thing he begged the troops for. They had beaten him nearly unconscious in our living room. Blood from his nose and eyes dotted the yellow walls and streaked the chair he used to sit on when he came home from work. Still, he begged them: "I will walk out on my own two feet. That is it. That is all I want from you." The second thing: the flyers they found did not belong to my father; they were mine. They were not found in his office, but in his bedroom, where he had taken them the night before, after he had found them in my room. That was partially why the soldiers beat him so thoroughly. He had refused to tell them where the flyers had come from. Eventually he said they were his. Of course they didn't believe him, but that was never really the point anyway.

The flyers were inconsequential. All they had was an acronym, SFD (Students for Democracy), and a time. There wasn't even a location on the flyer. When my father said the flyers belonged to him, my mother made a desperate attempt to throw her body over his, but the soldiers were well practiced in handling situations like this. I remember the studied, almost bored air in which they conducted the whole affair. They saw her coming long before she even took her first step. One of them simply raised the butt of his gun and leveled it directly at her chest. He didn't even have to turn around to see her coming. When she fell, it was as if someone had lifted her legs from under her, and then pushed her backward while she was in midair. She seemed to float across the living room, light as air, and just as inconsequential. And me? Where was I during all of this? Standing in a corner holding my seven-year-old brother's head against my body. As soon as the soldiers entered the house, my father had made a point of telling them that they lived there alone with their two sons, ages seven and twelve. I was small for my age back then. Small and skinny, without even a trace of facial hair, and a voice that still broke, especially when I was frightened. I had volunteered to pass out flyers to people I could trust. I was only sixteen at the time. I didn't believe in consequences yet.

The bedroom is a wreck now. I've forgotten the importance of maintaining order. The letters are scattered around me in a semicircle that begins chronologically and dissolves into carelessness. Hasn't this always been my problem? My uncle would say yes. He would say that I lack the ability to maintain structure and order. Begin from the beginning, he would say. Begin there, and then you can move on with your life point by point. That's why he has boxes full of letters, neatly arranged and tucked away, while I don't have so much as a picture of my own that dates back more than ten years. I never could find the guiding principle that relegated the past to its proper place. I can step in at any moment and see the house exactly as it looked that day, with the midafternoon sun spilling in through the front windows. My father has already seen and heard the soldiers coming and is waiting for them in the doorway. "Stay right here in the living room, together," he says. "Don't make them go looking for you. I'm sure everything will be fine." The guard who used to sit at the front gate of the house has already quit (as have all the other servants, and so maybe I should start there, with the day they emptied out their quarters and begged my mother and father to forgive them for having to leave). The truck carrying the soldiers simply rolls past the open gate and pulls up in front of the house. My father tries to greet them courteously. Unfortunately for him, he's wearing a suit that morning. He hasn't gone near his office in two weeks, but today he's decided to go and see what's become of it. Of course he knows already that all the windows have been smashed in, and that his files, or what remains of them, are littering the floor. (Or is this where the story begins, with my father's work as a lawyer?) Only three soldiers get out of the truck. There are at least four more waiting in the back. The lead soldier has a mustache, just like my father's. Neat, well trimmed, it arcs around his fat upper lip and stops just an inch above his pointy, hairless chin. He pushes my father into the living room with one hand. It's an important gesture, and in its own way could signal the start of an entirely different approach to this story. He already considers my father weak, vulnerable. The two soldiers behind him are carrying their rifles over their chest. They both have faint traces of facial hair, but they're still too young to grow a complete mustache. They can't be more than a year or two older than I was. My father tries to mention the names of high-ranking army officials he's known his entire life: Colonel Getachew Woldermarian, Captain Sisay. (That would be the wrong story, my father's early disillusioned days in the military. He was too slight and soft-spoken a man to have ever made a proper soldier.) The lead soldier sneers at the names (my father doesn't know yet that these men are all already dead or in jail). Then he spits onto my mother's carpet. That's the breaking moment. Regardless of how I get here, everything unfolds straight from that point, with no room for deviation or digression. As soon as he spits, one of the soldiers steps to the front and, with the butt of his rifle, knocks my father across the head. Is it possible that they practiced this routine before coming over? Or is it something that's grown organically out of their previous experiences? Spit and then hit. The two soldiers take turns kicking my father in the head and ribs. When my mother begins to cry out, the lead soldier draws his pistol and orders her to stop. She does so immediately. She's a strong woman, and nothing I ever say or do could describe or match that strength. He returns his gun to his holster and goes searching through the bedrooms. He's learned this from experience. Bedrooms are where people hide the things they want no one else to know of. We can hear him opening drawers. Glass shatters uselessly, unnecessarily, from somewhere in the house. It doesn't take him long to find what he's looking for, if in fact he's come looking for anything. (I know now that they would have taken him regardless, but things weren't so clear then.) When he returns with the flyers, my mother, who is now standing next to me in the corner, whispers one word to me: *"Zimbe."* Shut up. Close your mouth. Don't speak. It all comes to the same thing. The lead soldier taunts my father, who is now sitting up against the wall, with the flyers. He knows that they cannot have anything to do with a man my father's age, but he berates and hits him nonetheless. Where is this meeting and Who gave you this and Who are these people and What is your role with this organization and Who do you think you are and Who else is helping you and What are their names and What do you hope to accomplish with your meetings and Don't you know that this is a time of revolution and that there can be no room for dissension? My father's left eye has already swollen shut. He is struggling to keep his head from falling. He barely responds to the smacks that follow each ridiculous question. He begins to declare over and over that the flyers are his. The first tears are beginning to fall down his face. I found them and brought them home to throw away, he says, his voice cracking as he struggles for breath. Of course his pleas lead to more kicking, but at this point, my father has resigned himself to everything except claiming ownership of those flyers. He doesn't speak again until one of the soldiers bends down and reaches for his legs. It's only then that he begins to demand that they take their hands off him, as if somehow he had sanctioned everything they have done to him thus far. He lifts himself off the ground by bracing his back against the wall and climbing up with his entire body, inch by inch. His effort to stand on his own invites the mockery of the two young soldiers. They applaud sarcastically. They encourage him to go on. I pray to God, with as much conviction and faith that I have, for their deaths. I beg Him silently to kill them right then and there. I implore Him. I demand it of Him. If He cannot give me their deaths alone, though, then I ask Him to take all of us together. I pray for the roof of the house to cave in, for the ground to open up and swallow us whole, anything to end this moment.

I've never felt a disappointment so close to hatred again.

It takes my father at least ten minutes to stand. In what could pass for an act of mercy, the lead soldier tells his men to leave my father alone as he lurches his way off the ground. Of course, my father looks back one last time at my mother, brother, and me before he's escorted at gunpoint out the door. I'm not even sure how much he was able to see at that point—whether our faces were distinguishable from one another, or if through the haze of tears and blood the three of us merged into one indeterminate figure. I like to think that's the way he saw us, his family, not as individual people, but as a world, one that he could faithfully claim to have created. He couldn't have seen Dawit's face. It was buried entirely in my chest. Or my own, as most of it was hidden behind my mother's back. All of that is irrelevant, though. He didn't turn around so he could see us, but so that we could see him. He always believed in making a lasting impression.

The next day, at my mother's insistence, I left home. I took nothing with me but a small red cloth sack stuffed with all of the gold and jewelry my parents owned. I pawned and traded each item in order to make my way south to Kenya. By the time I crossed the border, the only I item had left were my father's cuff links.

10

The day after our evening tea session, Judith brought dinner to the store—a rosemary lamb roast with baby potatoes that we ate on paper plates with our hands, and a bottle of red wine that we drank out of six-ounce clear plastic cups. Looking back, it's possible to parcel our relationship out into distinct phases, the last of which began with that dinner. We had fumbled our way around each other long enough, and that meal was, I know now, our last opportunity to get it right.

Judith came to the store early that morning with Naomi, and this time she was the one who asked me what my plans for dinner were later that evening.

"If you're not doing anything," she said, "I could make dinner and bring it to the store. It'll be like a picnic, except of course it's winter, and we won't eat outside, but other than that . . ."

"I can't imagine anything better," I told her.

That was the only time either one of us spoke directly to the other about what we wanted. I almost regretted being so up front until I saw her smile at my response. There's something physical that changes with a person's appearance when they suddenly open up to you. For Judith, that change occurred almost exclusively in her eyes, which generally never rested for too long on any one person or object, unless it was Naomi. Now, though, she met my eyes with hers and did not back down.

I closed the store early for the third time so that we could eat our food before it got too cold. I pulled down the metal grate and turned the blinds and shut off the fluorescent lights. We used the lamp that I kept behind the counter and lit a row of tea candles that until then had been covered in dust. The light gave the store a warmth and glow that I had thought of as being reserved exclusively for homes.

We talked about Dostoyevsky and *The Brothers Karamazov* over dinner. Naomi and I spent a few minutes working out the pronunciation of the characters and author.

"Fee-a-door," I told her. "Like Theodore."

"Or fee at the door," Naomi offered.

"Yes. As in, from now on you have to pay a fee at the door before you can come and read in my store." Naomi shook her head and tried not to smile at my terrible joke, but I stared at her with my arms open until finally she relented and laughed even as she continued to shake her head.

"He was in jail once, wasn't he?" Judith asked me.

"Briefly," I told her. "After he was arrested he was carried into the city square, where he was supposed to be executed. They had the nooses all set, and it wasn't until the last moment that it was revealed to be a hoax. He spent four years in jail after that."

Naomi had a hard time understanding that story. She asked us why the government would do that to someone. Judith tried to explain to her that governments were no different from people, and that what they wanted, more than anything else, was to protect themselves. "Dostoyevsky," she said, "was a threat to them, and they wanted to get rid of him without having to kill him." Naomi couldn't understand that either, though, how one man could threaten an entire government just by writing.

"Maybe he couldn't," I told Naomi. "But somebody out there could, and until you know who it is, it's better just to scare everyone."

Our answers still weren't enough. There was a logical "why?" that could be attached to every response we came up with, and it seemed too harsh to say that terrible things happen to people for no reason other than they have to happen to someone. Finally Judith gave in and admitted what we had both been thinking.

"I don't ultimately know why," she said. "It's just one of those things about life."

Naomi accepted this answer, I suspect in part because she had heard it before. There was enough resignation in Judith's voice and enough resilience and determination in her daughter's to arrive at the truth, to make it clear that they had had conversations that ended like this one before.

After dinner we drove to the Mall in Judith's car to see the National Christmas Tree. It was Judith's idea. She said she wanted to see something that reminded her that Christmas was just a little more than a week away. There were hundreds of spectators surrounding the tree when we arrived, as if they were all expecting it to do something more than just stand there and twinkle in the darkness. I lifted Naomi into the air a few times so she could get a better view. Judith slipped her arm into the crook of my elbow and the three of us circled the tree once, and then twice.

When we returned home from the Mall, Judith invited me in for one last cup of tea. Naomi still had at least another hour before she had to go to bed and so she tugged on my arm and said in her high-pitched, pleading voice, "You have to come and see our tree."

Judith had gone out of her way to create an elaborate Christmas pageantry in their living room for her daughter. The dining-room table had been pushed to the side to make way for a seven-foot tree that glittered obscenely in white lights. Two stockings with embroidered names were nailed to the mantel. More lights framed the back window, and stacked under the tree were three enormous boxes. Each was elegantly wrapped in green, white, and red, with a huge red bow tied to the top.

"Those are all from Naomi's dad," Judith said, pointing toward the boxes. "He likes his presents to be . . . ostentatious."

I stared at the boxes and tried to guess their contents. It was obvious just from looking at them that whoever Naomi's father may have been, and regardless of how far away he may have lived, he had me beat.

"And what about you?" I asked Judith. "What do you like?"

"I prefer simple and elegant."

"I like small and cheap," I said.

"That's too bad," Judith said. "It looks like you've gone and picked the wrong family."

She said it without thinking, which I suppose was precisely what made it even worse. As soon as she said it she caught the look on my face and tried to take it back.

"Why did you say that?" I asked her.

"It was a joke," she said. "You know what I mean."

And I believed her; it had been a joke, but whether or not she meant it with the lightest intentions didn't matter. I could see myself trying to measure up at family dinners and cocktail parties, and as a result, always falling short. How many times would I have to stare into a mirror and compare myself against Judith? I could go on second-guessing myself forever, and perhaps even find some consolation to the routine, but I saw now that all it would take was one fleeting moment of skepticism on her end to confirm all of my inadequacies, validate all of my doubts, and send me running back to the corner I came from. Our insecurities run far too deep and wide to be easily dismissed, and Judith, without knowing it, had hit that central nerve whose existence I was reluctant to admit, but that when tapped, sent a sudden shock of shame and humiliation beneath which everything else crumbled.

She tried again to recover. "Come on, I'm kidding," she said.

Regardless of how hard she tried, there was no way she could take it back completely. I turned my head away from her. Naomi came up to me and led me by the hand to her presents.

"In here," she said, pointing to the green box, "is a TV for my bedroom. And in here is a dollhouse from Germany. I don't know what's in the white one because that's supposed to be a surprise."

"Germany?" I said.

"That's where he is right now," Judith responded. "He's teaching economics at a university there. Last year it was Greece, and the year before that Nairobi."

"So he's a professor?"

"That's how we met," she said. "He was a visiting professor from Mauritania."

The picture was complete now. I could see him, Judith's former husband and Naomi's semiabsent father. I imagined a tall, sandy-skinned man with oval wire-rim glasses and smart, well-tailored suits like the ones my father used to wear. Someone who spoke with a crisp accent, whom women described as being gorgeous. I imagined academic conferences, family vacations on windswept beaches, and late-night dinner parties. A confident and assured voice that knew how to order wines, talk to salesclerks, and command the attention of a room. Someone I knew I could never stand against.

I took another look around at Judith's living room, with its oversize Christmas tree and absurdly lavish presents. If what Judith wanted was another African to substitute for the one who had left her, then she was right, she had chosen poorly. I was not that man.

The teakettle began to whistle in the kitchen. It had a distinctive whistle to it, a singsong quality that was supposed to resemble, I imagine, an early morning birdsong.

"The tea's ready," Naomi said.

Judith walked over to her daughter and wrapped one arm protectively around Naomi's neck. Naomi clasped her mother's forearm to keep her from holding her too close.

"I think I should leave now," I said.

Judith tried to hide her shock but a fraction of it was still there, if not entirely in her voice, then at least in the way she quickly turned her head up to look at me.

"You just got here. What about the tea?" she asked me.

"Maybe another time."

I hated every word I said. Even as I spoke them I began the long process—one that would continue throughout the rest of that evening—of creating a series of different scenarios, ones that had me drinking tea on the couch and kissing Judith in the hallway. I couldn't bear being in that living room any longer, stuffed as it was with relics of Judith's former life, all of which pointed conclusively to distances too great to be crossed by a couple of dinners and over-the-counter banter. I wanted to take it back and start all over again, just as we had that evening in my apartment, but I knew that we had run out of roles to play.

"I'm sorry," I said. "But it's getting late."

"It's only nine o'clock," Judith pointed out.

"I know. But I have to wake up early tomorrow."

"Okay, then. If that's what you want."

Judith was not one to beg, but of course I wish she had. Perhaps then I could have set aside enough of my injured pride and self-pity to stay. I picked my coat up off the couch. The teakettle whistled on. Judith stopped watching me. She focused all of her attention on her daughter. I put my coat on quickly. How were we supposed to say good-bye now? With a hug or handshake or a quick wave like casual acquaintances? Judith settled the question by sticking her hand out. I took it, and in doing so learned what it meant to feel your heart break.

"Good night," she said.

"Good night," I replied. "Good night, Naomi."

"Good night, Mr. Stephanos."

I let myself out. I walked down the steps, straight toward the circle. I took a seat on a bench across from General Logan. It was cold and only a few people were out. A group of teenage boys walked past me. They turned their attention to me briefly, but once they recognized me for the harmless man I knew myself to be, they moved on. Finally, after close to thirty minutes of sitting in the cold, a group of women in short black miniskirts and stiletto heels walked by. I had never cared too much which of the women on the circle I went home with. I don't know how many women there had been over the years. I imagine it was somewhere between six or seven a year. Given the neighborhood and the location of my store, there was a simplicity and convenience that made each encounter seem almost logical, if not inevitable. I had slept with almost every prostitute who had come into my store. I did so by refusing to take their money when they came to the register to pay for their candy bar or can of soda. I would tell them that if they were free, they should come back alone just before I closed. When they did, I turned off all the lights, locked the door, and for a half hour tried to forget everything about myself. It was easy enough.

I stood up from my bench across from General Logan. I had settled on the woman walking closest to me. As soon as the women saw me standing up, they banded together. It was a small, protective act, just enough to make me sick of myself.

"Looking for something tonight?"

The voice that asked the question remained faceless in the dark.

"Sorry," I said. "I was just walking home."

I turned around and walked away in the opposite direction. The last thing I wanted to do now was scare anyone. I walked quickly, and had the streets been entirely empty I would have run away from the circle as fast as I could.

I I

When I first came to this apartment, my uncle sat me down on the couch in the living room and proceeded to lecture me about what I could expect to find now that I was in America.

"Everything that is in this apartment," he said, "belongs to you as much as it does to me. Outside of this apartment, though, you have nothing. Nothing is yours. Nothing belongs to you. Take nothing for granted. No one here will give you anything for free. There is no such thing as that in America. People will only give you something because they think they will get something in return."

I remember there was absolutely no passion or conviction to his words. He seemed to be reading them off an invisible monitor lying just before his eyes, aimed toward the ground as they were. I don't know if he saw in me a flicker of ambition or desire, but he need not have worried. I didn't want anything from America.

In those days I believed it was only a matter of weeks or months before I returned home to Ethiopia. I spent all my energy and free time planning for that. How was I supposed to live in America when I had never really left Ethiopia? I wasn't, I decided. I wasn't supposed to live here at all.

I nodded my head obediently as he spoke and pitied him for not understanding just how temporary all of this was.

For the first three weeks I was here in this apartment I didn't speak to a single person besides my uncle, and even then our conversations were brief and strained. I rarely left the apartment, nor did I want to. Any connection, whether it was to a person, building, or time of day, would have been deceitful, and so I avoided making eye contact with people I didn't know, and tried to deny myself even the simplest of pleasures. I refused to acknowledge the charm of a sunset or the pleasure of a summer afternoon. If possible, I would have denied myself the right to breathe another country's air, or walk on its ground.

My uncle and I lived off the divide that separated our life in this apartment from everything that occurred outside of it. I ate his food. I slept on his couch. For two months this was all I did. At the end of the second month he came into the living room while I was getting ready to sleep, and said in that always whispering voice of his, "*Buka.*"

I knew what he meant immediately: enough. And he was right, it had been enough. No one but he would have said it so gently, or granted me so much license.

I nodded my head in agreement. I was ashamed of myself and would have done anything he asked me to.

"Come with me to work tomorrow and I'll try to find you a job," he said.

That was how my life in America started. It seems a shame we don't know these things at the time. My first day of work at the Capitol Hotel, I was escorted by my uncle to the manager's office. My uncle introduced me as his nephew, Sepha Stephanos, although he told the manager he could call me Sepha, or even Steven for short, if he found that more convenient. The two men discussed my background while I stood there, mute. The manager, a solid, squat bald man whom I had been told to refer to only as "sir," didn't believe that I could speak English. He pointed to my skinny arms and asked my uncle if I had any problems lifting heavy objects, if I had any objections to working late-night shifts, if I could be trusted, in general, not to steal from the hotel or its clients. "No, sir," my uncle replied for me, "he has no problems. Perfectly honest. He has no objections to anything." The manager decided that I should begin that day so that he "could see what I was made of." He squeezed my right bicep once for good measure, and then held out his hand for me to shake. I remember wishing I had the courage and strength to crush every bone in his hand. After we walked out of the office, I heard my uncle mumble under his breath just loud enough so only I could hear, "Fucking bastard." Yes, it was a show of pride, halfhearted, but necessary nonetheless. It was one thing for him to "sir" his way through the day on his own, and an entirely different matter to have me there as a witness to it.

We rode the train back to Maryland together. We spoke as little as possible until we reached the apartment. When we reached home, I wanted to ask him if this was worth it: this one-bedroom apartment in a dilapidated building on the edges of a city. Our rent was only several hundred dollars a month, but look at what it took to earn that money. My uncle turned himself off every morning the moment he left the apartment for work. He didn't turn himself back on until ten or twelve hours later when he returned home. "Nothing" was the right word for the way he lived, and so was the vacancy with which he had said it.

I worked at the job my uncle found for me, and later on I attended the school he had picked. I hardly remember making any decisions of my own, until one night, three years later, when I realized I couldn't continue living like this any longer. The choice became clear to me as I walked alone along the banks of the Potomac after working two shifts at the hotel. My arms and legs were numb from thirteen hours of lifting luggage and bending at every moment to someone else's needs. It was too late at night to be walking alone along the empty riverbank, but there was nothing at that point that I cared for or worried about losing. Life could come or go and it wouldn't have made a difference. I walked miles that night, under the willow trees that had just begun to bloom. Lincoln's and Jefferson's memorials stood to my right, casting a distant pale glow over the river. I followed the Potomac to the Memorial Bridge and stood in the center, D.C. to one side, Virginia to the other. I leaned my body over the edge and stared down into the water wondering what, if anything, I had to live for. I couldn't believe that my father had died and I had been spared in order to carry luggage in and out of a room. There was nothing special to death anymore. I had seen enough lifeless bodies by that point to know that. I thought long and hard about what it would be like to simply step off the edge. I didn't know how to swim, nor would I have tried.

The next day I quit my job at the Capitol Hotel. I left my uncle's apartment less than a year later. They were the first real decisions I had made on my own since coming to this country. I loved them. Their impracticality made me love them even more. When I first told Joseph and Kenneth that I was leaving the hotel, they looked at me dumbstruck for a few minutes until Joseph finally leaned over and smacked my hand high in the air.

"You see, Stephanos? I always knew you had more in you. Soon we will all leave this place and the next time we come back, they will be carrying our luggage up the stairs."

Finding an apartment in Logan Circle was easy enough at the time. There was a "For Rent" sign in just about every building I passed. As for the store, that had been Kenneth's idea. "Be your own boss, man. That's the only way to get anywhere in this country." And so with Kenneth's help I got a small-business loan from the government. I opened my store in a space that had once been a liquor store. As far as I know, it was the first liquor store in the neighborhood to have gone out of business. Kenneth taught me how to keep track of my accounts, make lists, order supplies and goods, and balance my budget. I used to think he would have made an exceptional father, patient as he always was with me, and who knows, perhaps someday he will. In the meantime those fatherly instincts of his have led him into countless hours of tedious arithmetic, most of which I failed to learn properly. Joseph, for his part, came up with the name: Logan's Market. I've never heard anyone but him refer to it as such. For the store opening, he insisted on designing leaflets to pass around the neighborhood.

Logan's Market. A New Community Store to serve all of your needs. Carrying freshly stocked produce, canned goods, and general household needs at GREAT PRICES!

In his usual fashion, he toiled over those two sentences for an entire afternoon in my apartment.

"What do you think about this, Stephanos? Logan's Market, a leader in top-quality produce. Or better yet, Logan's Market, serving you and your family with only the freshest ingredients for the best prices."

His ideas only grew larger as he spoke.

"Logan's Market, an internationally recognized leader in top-quality products."

When I pointed out to him that his last suggestion might be taking it a bit too far, he responded with one of his twists of logic.

"Where are you from?" he asked me.

"Ethiopia."

"And what about me? Where am I from?"

"Zaire, Congo. Take your pick."

"Well, then. That settles it. If you ask me who has the best products, I will tell you Logan's Market. I am international, and so are you. That means the store is internationally recognized. It's all about marketing," he said. "You have to learn to think now like a businessman."

I let him scribble away in my apartment until he settled on something that matched the eloquence he knew he was capable of. By the time the store opened, Joseph and Kenneth had put as much energy and thought into it as I had. Kenneth was waiting for me in front of the store with a bottle of champagne the morning I opened.

"Don't you have work?" I asked him.

"I took the day off," he said. "I wanted to be here for this."

We drank the bottle later that evening once Joseph got off work.

"This is the beginning," Joseph said. "Today, right here with Stephanos's store. We begin new lives. No more of this bullshit. Right?"

We were all guilty of hyperinflated optimism and irrational hope at that point. But how could we not have been? You should have seen us then. Joseph was right, you wouldn't have believed your eyes. We were young, and we were skinny, and in our eyes beautiful. Joseph and Kenneth were both still working at the Capitol Hotel as waiters in the hotel's main restaurant, and the opening of my store—"our store," as we referred to it that night—was supposed to signal a departure from frustrating, underpaying jobs and unrealized ambitions. As that first night in the store wore on, our conversation grew increasingly grand, our ambitions and desires for the world limited only by imagination.

"You know, Stephanos, together we could be onto something."

That's Kenneth speaking now. He's raising his glass in the air, as if he's about to toast the sky, leaning back in his chair with the same repose that I've now come to know as intimately as my own gestures. In his own particular way, he could be just as hyperbolic in his speech as Joseph, even if he has a hard time accepting it. Now when he speaks it's always with an overly deliberate reserve and skepticism. He says it's because he's an engineer, but I know that's not it. I spent two months living in his oversize, barely furnished apartment when the heat in mine broke during the middle of a winter storm three years ago. I tried not to be around when he came home from work. I couldn't bear the sight of him sitting frozen and lifeless in a plastic lawn chair by the patio windows drinking beer after beer, wiggling his toes in his expensive wool socks. I came home one night and found him laughing hysterically to himself. The only light in the apartment came from the streetlamp that hung just a few feet away from the porch windows. It wasn't enough light to see him by, which was fine because I could hear him laughing and arguing with himself and I wouldn't have wanted to know what his face looked like while he was doing that. All of this would come about years later, of course, leaving that first night in the store to sit and burn in my memory.

"I mean, if we look at this store as the first step to an even greater venture . . . This neighborhood has potential, man. I tell you. We should begin thinking about expanding. In a year or two, you could have an entire grocery store. Start your own franchise." Kenneth sketched out some numbers on the back of a notebook. What did the numbers mean? Nothing, but they were nice to look at.

Joseph laid out his plan that night for getting his college degree and then his PhD from the University of Michigan.

"It's all very simple," he said. "I have talent, and top universities need talent. When they see what I can do they will beg me to come. I'm certain of it."

"And why Michigan?" Kenneth asked him.

Joseph scratched the bottom of his chin.

"Because it's a top-notch school. I knew a woman who went there once. She was a teacher. Smartest woman I ever met. She told me I was brilliant. 'Joseph,' she said. 'You are one of the smartest men I have ever met.' She told me I should go there someday, and that is what I am going to do."

Kenneth, for his part, was going to get his engineering degree and then a master's.

"Only then," he said, "will I go back to Africa. I will go to Nairobi in the finest suit and everyone will say, 'Look at him. That is someone important. That is someone special.' I'll build them buildings that will blow them away. No one will have seen anything like them."

As for me, I was going to sit in my high-backed chair behind a counter and read as silent as a god until the world came to an end.

❦

How did I end up here? That seems like an appropriate question to ask after seventeen years in a country. How is it that I came to own and run a store in the center of a blighted neighborhood, and how is it that now as my store, or what's left of it, is about to be taken away, that I can do nothing but sit on the floor of my uncle's apartment and run through the past? Narrative. Perhaps that's the word that I'm looking for. Where is the grand narrative of my life? The one I could spread out and read for signs and clues as to what to expect next. It seems to have run out, if such a thing is possible. It's harder to admit that perhaps it had never been there at all. Do I have the courage to explain all this away as an accident? "Do something," Kenneth admonished me earlier. That's precisely the problem, though, Kenneth. Once you walk out on your life, it's difficult to come back to it.

I wonder what's left of the store now. Two hours have turned into nearly five. The morning is gone, and so is the afternoon. Had I still been behind the counter, I would have been hoping for a rush-hour crowd that would never come. Yes, a handful of steady and loyal customers would have stopped by, as much to say hello and chat for a few minutes as to buy anything, but in another hour or two they would have gone as well, and I would be faced with the prospect of staring into an empty store, as poorly stocked and nearly as dirty as the day I found it.

I pick up the phone sitting next to the bed and call my store one more time. I dial the first four numbers and hang up. I pick the phone back up a few seconds later. I remind myself that I have nothing to lose anymore.

"I have nothing to lose," I tell myself.

I dial the numbers once more. The space between the last

number punched and the first ring is the hardest. Each ring seems elongated, and yet each pause isn't long enough. There are three, and then four rings. On the fifth ring someone picks up.

I hear a man's voice laughing in the background. It has an old, gravelly quality to it, the kind that comes with age and poor health. Another voice, younger, feminine, asks, "Who you talking to?"

It's one of those simple questions that at the right moment hits too hard. I hang up before whoever is holding the phone to the air can answer.

I scoop all of my uncle's letters off the floor and lay them back into the box in as close to the order I found them as I can manage. I take the lockbox, with all of the money he has saved, out of the closet and place it gently onto the floor. I lift open the lid, which is flimsy and serves no purpose at all. There is more than a thousand dollars in here—enough money to pay one month's rent on the store, buy a ticket home to see my mother and brother. It would be so simple to take the money, which is stacked in three clumps a few inches high and wrapped tightly in rubber bands. I could leave a note in its place, one that would explain, in as few words as possible, my reasons and failings. The note could say simply, "I'm sorry," or, "Forgive me." If I did that, I wouldn't even have to go through the trouble and disgrace of lying for it. I could simply take the money and run.

I shift the clothes on the floor of the closet back into place and return the lockbox delicately back to the corner I found it in. The thing to do now is to remove any trace of my having been here. My uncle will come home soon, and he will look around, never knowing that just a few moments earlier I had been here ready to take him for everything he had.

12

I couldn't bear to open the store the morning after I abruptly left Judith's house. That night after I left, I dreamed of standing side by side with a faceless woman whose name I never knew. We were on top of a hill, and she had her back to me, but we were together, at least that much was clear. There was a moment near the end of the dream when I nervously put my arms around her waist, and she leaned back into them. I woke up then with an overwhelming sense of loss, and I knew exactly where it came from. Instead of opening the store I stayed in bed until noon with the shades tightly drawn.

Mrs. Davis came to my apartment early that afternoon to check on me. She knocked on the door and called my name—"Mr. Stephanos, Mr. Stephanos"— until I answered.

"Why aren't you at the store?" she asked me. "I went to go get some milk and it was closed."

"I'm sorry, Mrs. Davis," I said. "I didn't know. I have some that you can have."

I walked to my refrigerator and gave her the only carton I had. My sense of obligation to the store and the people who shopped in it hadn't quite died yet then, although I could begin to feel it slip away. I hadn't thought of the store once that morning since I made the decision not to open it, and if I had considered it then, I would have realized that had never happened before.

Mrs. Davis put her hand on my forehead and took the milk with the other.

"You sick?" she asked me.

"I suppose so," I said.

She offered to bring me tea and then soup, but I refused, first gently, then adamantly. I told her I had other things I needed to get back to. As soon as she left I returned to my bed and picked up my fantasy where I had left off. Any moment now Judith was going to ring the doorbell and I was going to apologize, and she was going to apologize. Soon, we were going to laugh the whole thing off as a terrible but minor misunderstanding. Greater and more unlikely things happened every day. People won the lottery. Trains jumped off tracks. Missing children were discovered. Why not this?

The next morning I opened the store a half hour late for no reason other than that I could. When I arrived I found Naomi sitting outside waiting for me.

"What are you doing out here?" I asked her.

"Where were you yesterday?" she asked me.

"I was sick," I said.

She was sitting on the one tiny step in front of the store with her chin resting in the palm of her hand.

"I waited for you," she said. "For a long time."

I knelt down in front of her. There seemed to be no end to the disappointment I could cause.

"I'm sorry," I said again for the second time in as many days. "I didn't know."

"Are you feeling better?' she asked.

"A thousand times better," I said.

I opened the store for the both of us. Naomi piled her coat and scarf and sweater in the corner and pulled her seat up to the counter.

"Can we read for a little bit?" she asked me.

"Of course," I said.

That morning I gave her the best performance I could muster. When someone came into the store, I stayed in character. In the shrill old voice of the monk, Father Zossima, I asked a woman I had never seen before for "Threeeee dollllars. Seventy-one cents." I even hunched my back to heighten the effect. Naomi sat on her stool and chuckled in delight.

We stopped reading shortly before noon. I went to the back of the store and pulled out a long string of Christmas lights and a miniature plastic tree. For the next two hours, we decorated the store. I climbed onto a stepladder and Naomi handed me the lights in stages. We wrapped them around the store and then turned our attention to the tree.

"It needs some ornaments, don't you think?" I said.

"Yes," Naomi agreed. I gave her some markers, colored paper, scissors, and glue, and she went to work making stars for the tree. Finally the school supplies I had bought years ago found a purpose, and perhaps so would have everything in the store if given enough time. Naomi cut and colored a dozen stars of various shapes and colors while I sat next to her and watched. I put on a tape of Christmas songs, and when the right song struck us, we sang along.

When Naomi finished making the stars we decorated the tree with the few lights we had left. We placed it on the counter next to the register and then stood in the middle of the store so we could enjoy the view.

"What do you think?" I asked her.

For my sake, she looked up at me and said, "It's wonderful."

That settled it for me. I wanted to give her more than just a plastic tree and a store ringed with lights. I took a colored piece of paper and pen and wrote a note to Judith.

> *Sorry for leaving before tea the other day. I wasn't feeling too well. I have some Christmas presents I want to give you and Naomi. Maybe I can drop them by your house later this evening?*
>
> Yours,
> Sepha

I folded the note twice and slipped it into an envelope. I wrote Judith's name across the front.

"Here," I said to Naomi. "Give this to your mother when you get home. I have a surprise for you later on."

"What does it say?"

"You'll see," I told her. "First, though, I have to close up and run some errands. I'll see you later this evening. I promise."

I didn't try to hide my excitement. I knew exactly what I was going to do now. Christmas was imminent, and this year, for the first time in many years, I was going to make it something special. I didn't know what I was going to get Judith and Naomi yet, but the fact that I was going to get them anything was enough. I counted the money I had in the register and in the safe I kept under the counter. It wasn't much, just a couple of hundred dollars that I had been saving for some indeterminate event. Still, I felt flush, not only with money, but with an overwhelming desire to participate in all of the rituals the holiday invited. I suddenly wanted to know what it felt like to be one of those shoppers who ambled from store to store in search of the perfect presents, the ones who would say, this is how much I care about you, and, this is how thoughtful I am. It wasn't a new year quite yet, but I thought of what I was doing as the start of a new tradition.

The only presents I had bought in the past seventeen years had been for my brother, Dawit. I had stopped sending him toys years ago, though, once I realized he was no longer a child but a teenager, and a stranger. I imagined my presents being received in Addis with a certain justified contempt, and so instead of packages stuffed with toy soldiers and robots, I sent Christmas cards full of empty promises to come home one day soon. Christmas was still three weeks away in Ethiopia. I wouldn't receive a call from my mother until then. Normally by that point, any possible nostalgia for the holiday would have long since passed. It had been easy to continue living on the Ethiopian calendar at first. I could still remember that Christmas fell twice a year, once in December and again in January, but as the years accumulated, it became harder and harder to remember that there were two halves to the narrative. Last year, I didn't remember to call home until it was already late into the evening. My mother sighed heavily into the phone when she heard my voice.

I thought you had forgotten, she said.

No. I was just tied up at work. No one here knows it's still Christmas.

I only have two sons.

I know.

And you only have one mother.

I know.

Then don't tell me what other people know.

This year was going to be different. I was going to celebrate Christmas twice, properly on both occasions. I had something in America that I had never planned or thought I would have before: the beginnings of a life.

I still had enough time to buy something for Naomi and Judith and to send presents home for my mother and brother. Everyone would be surprised by my thoughtfulness and consideration. My mother and brother would forgive me for my years of neglect and distance. In the card sent with the presents, I would tell my mother that if she needed anything, she could count on me. As for Dawit, I would tell him that too much time had passed, and that I was ready to do now what I should have done years ago, which was to be a brother to him. For Judith, I would purchase something simple and elegant. For Naomi, something that would encourage her already grown-up spirit, something better than a dollhouse from Germany.

I planned my afternoon excursion into the city. I had at least five hours until the stores closed. I wanted crowds, lights, and decorations, Christmas music piping through intercoms. I wanted to lose myself in aisles of clothing and furniture.

There were buses and trains that went to the massive shopping malls just outside of the city limits, but by habit I had become a walker now. There would be lights strung along the trees in Georgetown, and as I walked, I could watch the city fade into darkness and emerge on the other side of the night still alive and vibrant with last-minute shoppers like myself. If I was lucky, perhaps another light snow would begin to fall, something that would add a touch of ambience to the evening. Of course I thought of Dickens's Scrooge, coming to Christmas at the last minute after having seen the horrors of his life laid before him. I even allowed myself to think of Naomi as my own angel, if not of Christmas past, then at least of present and future. I was going to buy her something wonderful, something that neither her mother nor father would have ever thought of. It would have to be something that would last her a lifetime.

As I walked up P Street, toward Georgetown Mall, I was aware of the light spring in my step. It wasn't going to snow as I had hoped, but that was all right. I was enjoying the brightness of the day for what it was worth. It added a touch of warmth to the air: a crisp, fresh winter air perfectly suited to a brisk walk. There were crowds and traffic the entire way. I could keep pace with the G2 bus, which every few feet was forced to a grinding halt by a passenger or traffic light. I could make out the faces of every person in every car. None of them were going to arrive at any destination soon. They were going to be late for their dinners and their meetings. If I could have, I would have told each of them that it was okay. There was nothing to be done. This was the way the world worked. Some days you floated through, others you merely had to endure. P Street. Poor, narrow P Street. It was stretched to the point of breaking today. Even the sidewalks were crowded. People were spilling out of every store the street offered. Madame X's bookstore had a line at the register. The grocery store was being robbed of its carts by people who refused to carry their bags of food home. It's not often you have this vision of your world. Once, maybe twice a year, you see it only for its sheer, simple beauty. For a few blocks at least, I knew almost every person I passed. Familiar faces, all of them. This was one of time's quieter tricks. It slowly, but surely, sheered off the unfamiliar edges of your life. A couple of people said hello to me as we passed on the sidewalk. Most, however, walked quickly past without ever meeting my eyes. That was okay, though. They wouldn't have recognized that they were looking at a new man.

By the time I reached the stores of Georgetown, I had finished making a mental list of what I was going to buy for everyone. For my mother, a bottle of perfume. If she hadn't changed too much, she still had at least a dozen bottles lined up on her dresser like toy soldiers, and was still searching for the perfect one. I was going to find it. For Dawit, a crisp button-down white shirt. He was a university graduate now. He had, as our father would have said, to play the part right. The last photograph of him that I had seen came in the mail last year. He had the same build as our father. He already looked more like him than I ever would. It was as if nature had split our features in half so that I would grow up to inherit my mother's high cheekbones and petite nose, while he would have the bolder and stronger features of our father. He had a full, solid head, with the same thick, wavy black hair that my father had said made him a favorite of all the women. Whereas my chin rounded off delicately at the bottom, Dawit's was defined by clear, hard lines. I hoped that his chin would serve him well later in life. For our father, it had ensured a certain level of respect from people who might have otherwise tried to take advantage of his soft demeanor. I wondered if Dawit was as gentle as our father was. There was something to his eyes that suggested he had the potential to be. I wondered if he would whisper as our father did when he was angry, or if he would become the type of man whose eyes would well up with tears whenever he was overcome with emotion. Our father loved white shirts. His closet was full of them. If they were still there, then

Dawit could add this one to the collection, and if they were gone, then I hoped he would consider starting his own.

For Judith, a book. Something rare and remarkable. It would have to be historical. It would have to be about America and politics, and it would have to have at least a touch of poetry to it. After our first dinner together, I had searched for her name at the local library and then again at the Library of Congress. Judith McMasterson. Author of one book, *America's Repudiation of the Past*, and several dozen scholarly arguments that had titles such as "Tocqueville's Legacy on American Poetics," "Writing Against History," "Nineteenth-Century American Writers Search for Place," "Silencing America's Poets," "The Grammar of Poetic History." I read fragments from each one, including several chapters from her book. She was a harsh, passion-filled academic. She often wrote in the first person. She filled her arguments in with personal narratives and opinions. There was something even slightly pompous to her arguments, as if what she really wanted to say about American history through the course of all those pages was, "None of this is good enough." She had a fierce loyalty to Emerson, and to the nineteenth century in general. My favorite passage was at the end of the book. After four hundred pages of dissecting Emerson's essays and *Democracy in America*, Judith dedicated her closing chapter to an obscure French author, Gustave de Beaumont, whose greatest public legacy was as Tocqueville's literary executor.

Beaumont never achieved the fame and recognition of his longtime friend Tocqueville. He published only one novel to be translated into English, *Marie, or Slavery in America*. There is a fragmentary, discursive quality to the narrative that to my mind seems more fitting of the American liter-

ary spirit than anything captured by Tocqueville. Beaumont may not have even known just how radical his narrative was. The central questions of racial identity and
women's role in society lie at the heart of Beaumont's trou-
bled novel, as if he had divined the next one hundred years
of America's future and written this book as an explana-
tion to those who would someday dare ask, "How did we
end up here?" History, all too sadly, often works that way.
The first creative spirits of a generation are often forgotten,
or neglected by time.

Since meeting Judith I had read *Democracy in America*, a
collection of Emerson's essays, and even *Marie*, a novel I had to
search through three libraries to find. I can't say that I understood America any better for having done so. What I did understand was just how seriously Judith took all of America's
failures, and just how much she loved its heroes. She may not
have said it, but I think a few thousand lines of poetry and a
handful of novels redeemed the entire country for her.

Inside an old used-book store in Georgetown, I found a 1928
edition of Emily Dickinson's collected poems. Buying the book
meant skipping out on that month's gas and electric bills and
crossing my fingers and hoping for a steady flow of business
through the rest of the winter. But it was a beautiful book. A
hard red cover, and a spine that had held up perfectly over all
these years. It had only a fraction of the poems found in a modern collection of Dickinson's poetry, but that seemed all the better.
Each poem had its own page, a few of which were dog-eared and
lightly written on. I didn't think I could have done any better.

I saved Naomi's present for last. It was going to be a journal.

I knew that from the start. I wanted it to be a grown-up journal, the kind that came with nice unlined pages and a hard leather cover that would fade and soften with time. I imagined it would be the type of journal that would carry her through adolescence and straight into adulthood. She would guard it zealously. She would carry it from home to home, hide it under her bed, and carry it in her book bag whenever she knew she was going to be away from home for more than a night. I didn't know how to tell her that she should put everything into it, but it had to be said. All of this was going to pass so quickly that if she didn't begin to record it now, it would be impossible to do so later.

I found the journal and a nice fountain pen to go along with it. I went to a French café off the main road and tried out my inscriptions.

Dear Naomi,

I wanted to give you this journal for a number of different reasons. I had heard from Henry, my chauffeur, that you were looking for the perfect journal in which to record your thoughts.

Dear Naomi,

I wanted to give you something that you could keep for the rest of your life.

Dear Naomi,

As the smartest eleven-year-old in the world, I wanted you to have someplace where you could write down all of those brilliant thoughts of yours. This can be your secret place to say and write everything.

I settled on that last one, although before I wrapped the journal, I would white out the word "Dear" and replace it with a simple dash: "—Naomi."

✤

When I returned home from my Christmas shopping, armed with my bags of presents, I found a note waiting for me on the landing to my apartment.

Dear Sepha,

   Thank you for the letter. It was very nice of you to think of us. Unfortunately, Naomi and I are leaving early this evening to spend the holiday with my sister and her family in Connecticut. I'm sure we will see you again shortly after we return. I hope you have a merry Christmas.

   I'm sorry.

Best,
JM

I brought all the presents into my living room and laid them out on the floor one at a time. I didn't know what to do with them now. I had bought wrapping paper just before coming home. It was a last-minute decision. I was passing a pharmacy, and there in the window I saw the usual display of trees and lights and presents and fake snow with elves and a sleigh resting around it. I went in and wandered aimlessly through the aisles, listening to the Christmas music and watching people buy bottles of perfume and bags of candy. I don't know if there really are general moods of joy and happiness that can come with a season, but if I had been left all alone, I could have danced through those aisles for hours. It was only when I noticed that the security guards were beginning to lower the grates to the door that I settled on a package of wrapping paper to take home. It came in a pack of three. One was red, with images of Santa Claus on his sleigh, another was green with mistletoe, and the last, a medley of green, red, and white pinstripes. The saleswoman threw in a free box of bows to stick on top. She smiled cheerfully at me as she threw them into the bag, and again I felt the same way as I had in the aisles.

I sat on the floor and ripped open the wrapping paper. I decided that red was for Naomi, green was for Judith and Dawit, and the pinstripes were for my mother. I had never wrapped a present before, and now, I decided, it was time I learned to do so. I wanted each of the presents to come out looking like the boxes under Judith's tree, but the more I cut and contorted the paper to try to fit it around the hard edges of each box, the more I realized that was never going to happen. But I tried. For nearly four hours I tried. I went through the first two rolls of wrapping paper in just over an hour. A few times I came close to achieving the effect I wanted, but it wasn't enough for me anymore. I wanted smooth, flawlessly wrapped presents, just like the ones Naomi's father had sent from Germany. I had begun with the bottle of perfume for my mother. It was small, just barely larger than my palm, but that, I decided, was the problem. It was too small. I went through the presents one at a time and found the flaws in each. Judith's book was too thin. Naomi's journal was too squat and with a pen wrapped on top formed an unnatural bulge that could never be wrapped properly. Dawit's box was simply too big. I spent most of one roll on his present alone. None of them fit the wrapping paper the way I needed them to. I tried measuring out pieces of wrapping paper to fit each individual side of each box. There was always something a little off: a corner would be showing, or another corner would have too much paper. If I clipped the extra piece of paper protruding from the edge, I would suddenly have too little, or I would find a sharp jagged edge sticking out. The edges were always the problem. Every flat surface was perfect. It was only when I tried to get around the corners that I got stuck.

By the time I ran out of wrapping paper, it was a few minutes past one in the morning. It didn't matter. The presents weren't going anywhere. If I had enough wrapping paper, I could have toiled away on my floor for another week, and there wouldn't have been any consequence. No one expected anything of me.

I tried stacking the boxes on top of one another in the hope that, taken together, they would lose some of their tattered, deformed quality. I set them on top of the coffee table and took a few steps back. Distance did nothing to redeem them. They looked nothing like the presents under Judith's tree. They looked as if they had been wrapped by a blind, one-armed man who had torn away at the wrapping paper and tape with his teeth.

Before going to bed I decided to take a walk around the neighborhood. I walked past my store and a few blocks farther south where there were still boarded-up buildings and glass-strewn sidewalks. A few people were out, mainly bored teenagers who sold drugs out of abandoned buildings and alleyways during the day. I wondered if the Christmas season was as good for their business as it was for mine.

It seemed like an appropriate night for walking down the middle of the street. I used to be afraid of this part of the neighborhood. As bad as things may have been around the circle when I first moved in, they paled against these blocks. Few people lived here. Half of the block was entirely burned out or boarded up. There was a unique fear that came with feeling that it was the inanimate objects around you that frightened you most. The crumbling brick façades streaked with black from fires that had raged decades ago didn't need rumors of violence to intimidate. They were frightening enough on their own. Like anything, they had softened with time. All I saw now was how sad and empty they looked—how sad and empty all of these blocks looked.

I cut through the circle before returning home. I sat on one of the brightly lit benches nearest the street and waited for the few women who still hung around the circle late at night to come by. This time it took only a few minutes of waiting before two walked by together. They slowed down as they neared me; one of the women recognized me from the store. There were familiar faces everywhere I went today. They drew nearer, and the woman I knew asked me if I could use a "special Christmas date."

"What do you say?"

I didn't hesitate. I stood up and said, "Yes." The other one walked away. I decided to go back to my apartment. It was late enough at night that I wouldn't have to worry about Mrs. Davis or any of my other neighbors watching me. Judith and Naomi had gone to Connecticut. I had nothing to lose.

We lay down on the couch first, and then later the bed. I wanted to be more than just half-present, which is to say I wanted to see myself fully and honestly, naked in my bed with a woman whose real name I would never know. I took pleasure in feeling another body under me and on top of me. I buried my head in her chest and treated her as if she were someone I loved. It was purely the context of the evening that mattered. It gave a certain weight and substance to what we were doing, so that when we were done and lying on my bed with the orange glow of the streetlamp as the only light in the room, neither one of us moved or rushed to get up.

Before she left, she asked me who the presents were for.

"I'm not sure anymore," I said.

"Nice wrapping job you did there."

The living room was littered with scraps of wrapping paper. I hadn't bothered or tried to clean any of it up before I left, and could have cared less about it when I returned.

I separated Dawit's present from the other three.

"Pick one," I told her.

"You don't care which one?"

"No. You can have any one of them."

She considered each box thoughtfully, without touching any. She pointed toward the bottle of perfume.

"Can I have that one?"

"Of course," I told her.

"What is it?"

"Perfume."

"I don't wear perfume," she said. "Gives me a headache."

"That's okay," I told her. "Just give it to someone you know."

13

I decide to take the bus from my uncle's apartment to see Joseph at his restaurant. There are buses constantly coming and going from in front of the complex, each one as crowded as the one behind it. Today it's standing room only on all the buses. The crowd is my consolation for not walking. The bus I'm on is the M28, while behind us is the M34 and in front of us is the M19. I may marvel at the trains, but it's the buses that have my heart. The trains speak to that part of me that craves to know that there is an unseen hand into which I can place if not my life, then at least my ability to move from one location to the next in the dark; the buses are a test of my faith in man. They go into the neighborhoods the trains don't dare to touch, sneaking down narrow side streets, squeezing in between cars and buildings. I was never allowed to ride the buses in Addis until I became old enough to do so without my parents' knowledge, but the city and country fell apart shortly after that, and so all I have are a handful of memorable rides taken alone through the city's haphazardly carved streets, past the tin-roof shantytowns that adorned everything but the richest neighborhoods. My mother, brother, and I were always carted from home to school to whatever event my father might have planned for the evening in a simple black sedan driven by either my father or, when he was away at work, the guard who always stood in front of our house while we were there. Inside our quiet car was a family, properly restrained, with music playing softly from the front. Occasionally my father whistled along to one of the sad Ethiopian pop songs that I still listen to. His tune filled the car to the exclusion of any other sound that might have tried to interfere, while outside on the bus a small, chaotic world orbited around the city. Compared to the crowded city buses that rolled through downtown Addis, my empty backseat seemed like such a hollow and lonely existence. Each window had a half-dozen faces pressed against it. Old women with their heads wrapped in a thin white cloth and children with their dirty rags and mud-stained faces stared at me through the windows, while standing above them were the faceless shirts and pants of men who eyed one another suspiciously and kept their money tucked into their hands. They hardly had space enough to breathe, much less move, and that was what I envied most. While I sat comfortably alone in the backseat of my father's car, there was an entire city moving together, block by city block, with every curve and bump the bus took through the pothole-riddled streets of the capital, like marionettes attached to the same piece of string being orchestrated by the bus driver's hands. I imagined the crowd exiting the bus through the windows and doors like water spilling out of a jar full of holes, and I imagined them entering much in the same way, except in reverse. I wanted to be with them. I would have given anything to have disappeared into one of those buses, swallowed whole by the crowd, my face and limbs so thoroughly merged into theirs that the words "I" and "alone" could never be uttered again.

When the revolution came the buses emptied out. During those first few months I would sometimes see one trolling down the street, empty with the exception of the driver and a few soldiers who stood near the windows, their guns pointing out. Later, the buses were used to carry hundreds of boys to one of the new prisons built on the outskirts of the city. I remember thinking that I couldn't understand how a city that had demanded so much intimacy could turn on itself. It was the thought of a childish, privileged young man, but that didn't make the disappointment hurt any less.

When I lived in Silver Rock with my uncle, I often spent my free Friday and Saturday nights hopping from one crowded bus to the next. I rode the buses until the crowds began to thin out, and then I would get off and take another crowded bus back in the same direction. Eventually I came to know which buses were the busiest at which times of day, which buses could be counted on to always arrive on time or full to the brim, and which ones always left me wanting more. It was enough to feel that for twenty or thirty minutes I had locked myself into the same fate with dozens of people who, like myself, could barely move their hands out of their pocket or shift their weight from one foot to the other without pressing against someone else. To me, the buses were the benchmarks of civilization, although at the time I would haven't known to describe them as such. Instead, I would have said that I felt safer on those buses than I did anywhere else in this city.

I have at least another hour before Joseph gets off work.

Joseph was proud of this job when he first started, although he could never have admitted it. Yes, he was still a waiter, but instead of working at a decent restaurant in a nice hotel, he was working at the "premier eating establishment of the District's elite." Those were his words: "This restaurant is the premier eating establishment of the District's elite." And it is. The Colonial Grill is where senators and lawyers and lobbyists go to dine for lunch and dinner. The restaurant is wrapped in glass and looks onto one of the busiest intersections of the city, so that at any given moment during the workday it's possible to spy on the city's "elite" conducting their affairs and those of the country over three-course lunches served on white tablecloths under crystal chandeliers and plastered ceilings. Joseph was forced to learn the names and faces of every regular politician who ate at the restaurant. He knows all one hundred senators and close to half of the House by sight alone. His first year at the restaurant, he reported to Kenneth and me at the end of each week whom he had served and seen. He always added a slight conspiratorial note to each narrative, convinced, as he was, that everything of any import happened with secret whispers and handshakes.

"You know who came in on Tuesday? The president's chief of staff. And you know who he was eating with? That senator from Mississippi that no one likes. They were the only two at the table. I watched them. Neither one of them laughed or smiled the whole time. That can't be good for things."

His interest in the city's politics lasted only as long as it took him to know the faces behind it. Once he accomplished that, there was no more mystery or surprise. Politicians came and went. They ate their lunches. They tipped generously. They demanded to be treated like royalty, and that was it. Perhaps Joseph had believed that his physical proximity to power meant great things were in store for him. That was what the Colonial Grill was supposed to have meant—a step up in the world, a sign of progress, advancement, promotion. When he first came to D.C., he had worked as a busboy, and then as a bellhop, and now as a waiter. We all have measures by which we gauge the progress of our lives. Joseph has been generous with his. It's been nineteen years since he came to America, and he has tried to see each and every one of those years in the best possible light. Michigan and the PhD are now the idle dreams of a restless young immigrant.

"You don't need a PhD anymore," he said to me once. "Anything you want to learn in this world, you can learn in this city for free." We were walking back from the Library of Congress, where we had spent most of an afternoon looking for the poems of an obscure Congolese poet Joseph remembered reading as a teenager. In his rare and sober off hours from work, he was working on his own cycle of poems, ones that would trace the history of the Congo from King Leopold to the death of Patrice Lumumba and the rise of Mobutu Sese Seko.

"The poems," he said, "are like the *Commedia*, except there is no heaven. They begin in hell, they come out for just a moment, and then they return."

Once, in his underfurnished and oversize studio, he read to me the last few lines of the first section, the one that ended with the departure of Belgium from the Congo and the rise of Lumumba as prime minister. The scene was his equivalent of Dante's "Some of the beautiful things that heaven bears."

We have come this far, to find we have even further to go
The last traces of a permanent twilight have faded and
   given way
To what we hope is nothing short of a permanent dawn.

"Those lines still need some work," he said. "I haven't quite captured the mood I want. I want the reader of this poem to know what it felt like to be in the Congo in nineteen sixty. It was more than just a new beginning. It was a brand-new world. It was like everyone in the country became a new mother and father at the same time. But I can't say that. Can I? No. I need something more subtle, less direct, but without losing any of the feeling."

As far as I know, Joseph is still working on those three lines two years later. Occasionally, when drunk, he brings them back up again.

"I think I've got them now, Stephanos. They came to me last night like a line from heaven:

Let us stop. Let us begin again.
Let us clean the blood from the rubber fields
And do what we promised to do."

Each incarnation has had a different theme and point of departure. One version of those lines was directed toward King Leopold. Another was told in the voice of a mutilated plantation worker staring at his severed hands lying in a basket already full of hands. And yet another was in the voice of an orphaned child witnessing the birth of a new nation. The last version he read to me was the sparest of them all. It simply went:

Patrice.
Are we ready?

The problem, Joseph said, was that he wanted to tell the entire history of the Congo, from the rubber plantations to the first coup. "Nothing can be left out," he said. "The poem must be able to contain it all. Anything short of that is a failure."

Those early lines of poetry gave Joseph just enough romanticism to make it through his years at the Capitol Hotel, and now the Colonial Grill, but they were losing their power. Now, when he talks about the restaurant, it's exclusively as a joke or sarcastic comment. He refers to it as the Colony. He talks about it only when he's sitting back comfortably in a chair, his legs crossed, preferably with a drink in one hand and a cigarette in the other.

"It was terrible at the Colony today. Absolutely terrible. The natives went crazy. We ran out of the risotto. The women were tearing off their pearls. The men were spitting in their wine. We almost had to teargas the place."

It's only a few minutes after five o'clock by the time I reach the restaurant, and already it's crowded. The Colonial Grill hasn't changed at all since I last saw it. I used to walk past it every day when I worked at the Capitol Hotel. Joseph and I would sometimes take our lunch break together, and when we did, we would walk past the restaurant and stare in through the huge glass windows that wrapped around the sides of the building and exposed it to everyone who stood or drove by the corner it sat on. Our translucent reflections were shot back to us as we watched the finely dressed men and women inside sip their water. Occasionally we mimicked the conversations that we imagined were going on inside.

"You know, Stephanos," Joseph would say, "this steak is rather dry for my taste."

"You don't say, Joseph. I was just thinking the same thing."

"This place is not what it used to be."

"No. You're quite right. But what can you do? The whole country is going to hell."

"Not just the country, Stephanos. The whole world is falling apart around us."

I spot Joseph from outside as he rushes back to the kitchen with another order waiting on his lips. I've never seen him fully dressed for work. Whenever he comes to the store, he always takes off his shirt and bow tie in exchange for the Michigan sweatshirt he wears on all but the warmest days.

On his way back to a table with three elderly white women situated around it, Joseph catches me staring at him through the windows. Our eyes meet, and for a few seconds neither one of us moves. He stands there frozen in the middle of a busy restaurant designed to look like a nineteenth-century English dining room, complete with enormous crystals chandeliers and red velvet drapes swooping in the corners of every window, while I'm fixed to my own stretch of the sidewalk, framed by the glass office towers behind me. We're both aware of the rush and noise surrounding us. Behind me is a line of cars waiting for the light to change and a steady flow of people walking to and from their offices, while surrounding him are tables full of people ordering their food and scraping clean their plates. Another waiter nearly collides with Joseph as he rushes by with his arm stacked with empty coffee cups and dessert plates. We could be old lovers reuniting the way we stare at each other, but instead we're two old friends who've known each other for years and yet can't seem to make sense of the image staring back from only a few yards away. Joseph barely looks anything like the man I know. It's not just the tuxedo that changes him, it's the context and the expression on his face. Despite what he may have said in the past, I've always known that he has never wanted Kenneth or me to set foot inside that restaurant while he was working there. I had never guessed that perhaps it was even too much just to see him. He tries to smile at me but the look comes across as forced. It's a grimace, not a smile, the type of expression you would give to someone whose offensive remark you try to go along with.

Another waiter deliberately nudges Joseph gently on the shoulder as he passes. He sets off for the table that had been his original destination, but he never takes his eyes off me and I never take mine off him. There is no denying anymore who we are and what we've become. I give him a simple wave good-bye just as he approaches the table of women, who are all looking at him, somewhat confused. He nods his head once toward me and then turns to the women. I watch him for just a second longer before rounding the corner and disappearing from his sight.

✤

There are fewer than twenty blocks now separating the Colonial Grill from my store in Logan Circle. I know these blocks as intimately as I know any other streets in this city. While so much has changed, these twenty blocks have remained obstinately the same. So, this is the city that I've made my life and home. It seems important now to think of it in that way. To consider it not in fragments or pieces, but as a unified whole. As a capital city, it doesn't seem like much. Sixty-eight square miles, shaped roughly like a diamond, divided into four quadrants, erected out of what was once mainly swampland. Its resemblance to Addis, if not always in substance, then at least in form, has always been striking to me. As a city, Addis wasn't much larger. Ninety square miles, most of which was a vast urban slum built around the fringes of a few important city centers. The two cities share a penchant for circular parks and long diagonal roads that meander and wind up in confusion along the edges. Even the late-afternoon light seems to hit D.C. the same way. Right now it's a soft, startling pinkish hue folded into a few large clouds building up along the western horizon. In two more hours, it will dissolve into long, dark red tendrils of light that will stretch across the sky, and this day will have finally ended.

The office towers fade quickly. They stop at a specific point, leaving the rest of the blocks ahead to the houses and stores that are neither completely run down nor well maintained, but somewhere perfectly in between, as if whoever lived in them had been asked by some higher power never to stray too far from their starting point.

I can't help but think of what I'm doing as going home. "I'm going back home." I say the words out loud as I turn left on Massachusetts Avenue, leaving the last of the city's downtown towers to itself. The sidewalks and street are thick with traffic. There is a simple and startling power to that phrase: going back home. There's an implied contradiction, a sense of moving forward and backward at the same time, but there's no tension in the phrase. Instead, the contradiction gives in to something else: an understanding, perhaps, that what you're returning to can never be the same as what you left. I understand now that distant, faraway look I've seen in other immigrants when they talk about returning to wherever it was they first came from. I can see my store exactly as I left it this morning. I can remember the exact location of my chair behind the counter, the amount of change in the cash register, the look of the aisles, and the way the light hit the windows. I can see all of that just as clearly as I can still see the look on my mother's face as she handed me all of her jewelry in a red cloth sack and begged me to leave. There she is with deep bags under her eyes, her long black hair tied in a loose bun, the white blanket she's wrapped herself in rising up and down with her deep breaths. It was less than twelve hours since my father had been taken away, and there we stood at the front of our house in the near perfect predawn blackness testing the merits of certain words over and over.

A trail of fire engines are stalled in the traffic on Massachusetts Avenue, their sirens wailing uselessly over and over as the cars in front of them search in vain for an inch of space in which to move. What will be waiting for me when I return? The cynic in me has already altered everything into an unrecognizable, chaotic mess. I picture my store burned to the ground, its contents looted. I imagine a crowd gathered around the charred remains of the building, shaking their heads silently in sympathy, in pity. Cans of Campbell's soup are rolling down the sidewalk and street. The air smells of melted plastic, and no one can do anything because the trucks sent to save my store are here in front of me moving at roughly the same pace that I am.

It would be so much easier never to return, wouldn't it? To just keep walking down this road until I hit the city's edge. And from there I could hop on a bus or train and make my way farther south, or north, and start all over again. How long did it take for me to understand that I was never going to return to Ethiopia again? It seems as if there should have been a particular moment when the knowledge settled in. For at least the first two years that I was here, I was so busy passing my mother, brother, father, and friends in the aisles of grocery stores, in parks and restaurants, that at times it hardly felt as if I had really left. I searched for familiarity wherever I went. I found it in the buildings and in the layout of the streets. I saw glimpses of home whenever I came across three or four roads that intersected at odd angles, in the squat glass office buildings caught in the sun's glare. I found a small measure of it in the circles and in the beggars who slept under the office towers at night. I used to let my imagination get the best of me. My hallucinations of home became standard. I welcomed them into my day completely. I talked to my mother from across the bus; I walked home with my father across the spare, treeless campus of my northern Virginia community college. We talked for hours. I told him about my classes, about Berhane and our little apartment together and my job carrying suitcases at the Capitol Hotel. I explained to him the parts of American culture that I had never heard of before. "There's no respect here," I told him. "The students in my class call our teacher John. They dress like they're coming from bed and then sleep through class."

I couldn't have asked for a better listener than my father. We talked and saw more of each other during my first two years here than in all of the years we spent living under the same roof. It was so easy to slip him into my day. All it took was a passing thought of him in his impeccable white shirt and pinstriped suit, and there he was. Does any of this make sense to you, *abaye*? I know you wouldn't have had much patience for these conversations with the dead. That would have never been your style. You would have simply asked that I remember you fondly. But it's nice having you here with me for just a little while as we near 13th Street. You would have loved this city on a day like today. You used to stretch open your hands and crane your neck back so you could feel the wind wrapping around you, a gesture that I can't help but mime every time a warm breeze blows by. Perhaps you would have thought, as I always do, that the portrait of Frederick Douglass painted onto the back of that red building on the corner bears, from the right angle, a striking resemblance to one of the pictures of Haile Selassie that used to adorn the walls of the capitol. I was saying earlier that I couldn't remember at which point I understood that I had left home for good. I can't seem to remember, either, when we stopped having these conversations. The two are connected, aren't they? I never understood that until right now: that everything went with you.

14

Christmas morning I went back to my store. I took down the "Closed" sign that I had put up the afternoon Naomi came to the store, and placed a chair in front of the register so I could read *The Brothers Karamazov* and stare absently out the window. I had decided to open up again out of a sense of obligation. Christmas, after all, was not a holiday that immigrant storekeepers were permitted to take. The world depended on us to work on Christmas day to provide last-minute supplies of groceries for dinner and batteries for new stereos and radio-controlled cars, not to mention the extra cases of beer and wine I always purchased just before the holiday season began. Christmas day was my favorite day of the year to work. Once I learned to forgive the faith, I began at least to appreciate the general effect the holiday had on people. There was a quietness to Christmas that I loved, an absence of sound that fell on Logan Circle with the force of a finger being pressed against a child's lips. On warmer and sunnier Christmas days, I would spend most of the afternoon standing right in front of the store, leaning back against the wall, just staring vacantly into the emptiness. There were no cars. There were no people on the sidewalk or in the circle. It felt as if the world had been abandoned by the people who had been busy making it and destroying it, and now the only ones left were timid shopkeepers like myself. Blessed are the meek, for they shall inherit the earth, if not for eternity, then at least for a few hours once a year. The customers who came to the store that day generally came in high spirits, filled to the brim with the Christmas mirth and alcohol that would keep them beaming for at least a few more hours. I met their high spirits with equally high spirits of my own, delighted, as I was, to have a day that could pass so pleasantly. I didn't worry about how much the store made that day. If it made nothing at all, I couldn't have cared less.

This was exactly the type of Christmas I loved the most. Sunny, slightly warmer than usual, with a few thin clouds to drift lazily over the sky for contrast. Perhaps it was the weather that brought out the steady stream of customers into my store over the course of that morning and afternoon. They came every ten to fifteen minutes for several hours. A few were from the neighborhood, but most were people passing through on their way to Christmas dinners with aunts, uncles, and in-laws they tried to avoid for most of the year. Aluminum foil was important that year. I must have sold as much of it in that one day as I had in the previous six months combined.

At six o'clock I called Joseph to see if he and Kenneth had any plans for the rest of the day.

"I thought you might be spending the day with your new lady friend."

"She's in Connecticut."

"I see."

"There's nothing to see."

"Don't be angry at me, Stephanos. I'm not in Connecticut. I'm here sitting by myself just like you."

"Where's Kenneth?"

"At work. Can you believe that? He said his boss asked him 'to take one for the team' and come in today. He was happy about it, though. He said it showed that they trusted him. Engineer or not now, he's a damn fool."

Joseph and I made plans to meet at our damp, sometimes crowded bar on the edge of the city in an hour. I would close the store early, while he would call Kenneth at his office and talk him into meeting us there. If all went well, the three of us would spend yet another Christmas night together, laughing at our isolation, mocking one another and ourselves for all we were worth until the night faded into a blurry, indistinguishable memory.

Since it was Christmas, I decided to take cab rides for the rest of the night as a present to myself. For most of the ride there, my cab was the only one on the road. The driver blew through traffic lights and stop signs, and he and I didn't say a word to each other. It was exactly the way I wanted it.

I beat Joseph to the bar, which was already half full by seven o'clock, a horseshoe of men perched on their backless stools around a wooden bar covered in alcohol. By the time he arrived, I was already several drinks into the night.

"You're drunk, Stephanos," was the first thing he said to me.

"Maybe a little."

"It doesn't fit you. You're too skinny. You look like you're about to fall asleep. It's those big eyes of yours."

"You should catch up."

"I've already had a bottle of wine. It was my Christmas present from work. Two bottles of cheap red wine that no one ever
orders."

"But you drank it anyway."

"Of course. I'm a man of taste, not means. I drank it and read
Rilke in German."

"You don't speak German."

"No. But I love the sounds. All those harsh *vert*s and *gert*s. It's
absolutely beautiful."

"Everything is beautiful to you."

"Not everything."

"But damn close."

"You just have to have the right perspective."

"Which is what?"

"Indifference. You have to know that none of this is going to
last. And then you have to not care."

"And then the world becomes beautiful."

"No. It becomes ridiculous. Which is close enough for me. So
what happened to you today?"

"Connecticut."

"What did you expect?"

"I don't know."

"That she would want to spend Christmas with you in that
neighborhood? The three of you crowded in your apartment
singing Christmas carols? Come on, Stephanos."

"Is it that ridiculous?'

"Yes."

"Okay. Then you understand."

By the time Kenneth joined us, Joseph and I had been sitting
at the bar for nearly two hours. He arrived dressed in his usual
work suit, his tie loosened just beneath the collar. He was tired.

His shoulders were hunched just slightly. His eyes had a weariness and vacancy to them that reminded me of the look you sometimes see on an injured child who has just caught a glimpse of something cruel and unfair happening to someone he loves. It was almost nine o clock. He had worked at least a twelve-hour day entirely alone.

"Look," Joseph said. "The man even wears a suit when he's the only one in the office. You're the perfect immigrant, I tell you. The INS should make a poster out of you, Kenneth. You could even be their spokesperson."

After a bottle of wine and half a dozen drinks, Joseph had finally managed to get drunk. He had grown practically immune to alcohol between the weight he had put on over the years and all the wine he drank during the off moments at his job. He was yelling and wagging his pudgy fingers at Kenneth as he spoke.

"I tell you, Kenneth. Ken. Had this been the eighteen hundreds, you would have been the perfect house nigger."

"Which one is it, Joseph?" Kenneth shot back. "The perfect immigrant or the perfect slave? You can't have it both ways."

"Says who? The engineer? Maybe in your world you can't. But in mine, everything is that way."

Kenneth turned his back on Joseph. He placed his arm on the bar to create a wall between Joseph and the two of us.

"How are you, Stephanos?"

"He's terrible," Joseph responded. "He wishes he were singing carols and celebrating Christmas in Connecticut."

"That would be better than listening to you right now. What happened? I thought you might be with that woman and her daughter."

"Judith and Naomi, you mean."

"Yes. I'm sorry. Judith and Naomi."

"They went to Connecticut," I said.

"Without you?"

"Yes. Without me."

"You ever find out about the little girl's father?" Joseph interrupted.

"He's a professor from Mauritania."

"Ah. Mauritania."

There was a wistful tone to Joseph's voice when he said that. *Ah, Mauritania.* The words had a certain rhythm to them, just like celebrating Christmas in Connecticut and the *vert*s and *gert*s of German poetry that he claimed to find so beautiful.

"They were French too, you know," Joseph continued. "I once had the pleasure of being told by a Mauritanian that he couldn't understand my Negro French. That's okay, I told him. *Ce n'était jamais à moi.*"

He paused for a second and smiled to himself as he admired his own wit. These were the parts of our conversations that he loved the most. I could see Kenneth preparing another question about Judith, Mauritania, and Naomi. Joseph caught the expression as well, and before Kenneth could press the matter any further, Joseph said, with a sly, ironic smirk, "Shall we begin?"

"I think we already have," I said.

"You're right. We have. Fine, then. Who do we have in Mauritania, Kenneth?"

"I don't consider Mauritania a part of Africa," Kenneth said. "To me, they are Arabs. They belong to the Middle East."

"So you don't know, then?" Joseph asked.

"No. I don't know."

"Stephanos?"

"Ahmed Taya."

"Not bad, Stephanos. And the year?"

"Nineteen seventy-eight?"

"Wrong coup. Try again."

"Nineteen eighty-one?"

"Wrong one again. One more try?"

"I give up," I said.

"Nineteen eighty-four. Just like the Orwell novel."

"Taya was the head of the army?" Kenneth asked.

"No. Just a colonel," Joseph said. "All the best dictators are colonels. Qaddafi. Taya. Both are still going. You have to respect that. A general would have never lasted as long. Even your Mengistu, Stephanos. He was a colonel."

"But he's gone now either way," I reminded him.

"The point is he did well for himself. You have to admit."

"You're right," I acknowledged. "Seventeen years isn't so bad. He even managed to kill a few generals along the way."

"You see? That's the thing about these colonels. They get just far enough to think they deserve it all. A general has already been close to the top. They become lazy lions up there. The colonels, on the other hand, never rest. They're too impatient. They know they don't deserve it. And so they last. Name me one colonel removed by his own army."

After a few moments of silence, Joseph declared triumphantly, "Exactly."

"How many does that make now?" Kenneth asked.

"At least thirty," I said.

"I wonder what we're going to talk about when we run out."

"We're never going to run out," Joseph said. "Having a coup is addictive. Look at what happened after Idi. Yusufu Lule, Godfrey Binaisa, the return of Obote, and then Tito Okello. One after another. Why would anyone want to stop? I wish I had been there to see Mobutu go. I would have been one of those people you saw dancing in the street. I would have carried Kabila on my shoulders straight to the president's palace if I were there."

Joseph finished his speech by leaning over the bar and snapping his fingers for another drink. As he leaned too far over the counter to catch the attention of the bartender, Kenneth abruptly stood up.

"Where are you going?" I asked him. "You just got here."

"Sorry, Stephanos. I'm tired of these conversations. I'm going to go home and sleep. I have to be back at work tomorrow."

"Let him go, Stephanos," Joseph said. "The Big Man is tired of our African talk. He wants to go home and dream of his new suit."

"What was your father, Stephanos?" Kenneth asked me.

"A lawyer."

"That's right. A lawyer. And you, Joseph?"

"You know what he was."

"A businessman."

"Yes. A businessman."

"And what was mine?"

Kenneth looked over at Joseph, and then me, knowing that neither one of us knew how to answer his question.

"Come, Joseph. I've told you this before."

"He was illiterate," Joseph responded.

"What else?"

"That's it."

"Exactly. That's it. That's all he ever was. A poor illiterate man who lived in a slum. And you know what that makes him in Africa? Nothing. That's what Africa is right now. A continent full of poor illiterates dying in slums. What am I supposed to miss? Being sent into the street to beg white tourists for money? If I die today, my sister in Nairobi will get one hundred thousand dollars. Someone would have to come and move the furniture out of my apartment. My suits will be shipped back to Kenya for my cousins. You, Joseph, would get my car. The only thing my father owned when he died was a picture of Jomo Kenyatta. His great leader. From the day I was born, there have been only two leaders of Kenya. The first was terrible, and now the second is even worse. That's why I'm here in this country. No revolution. No coup."

Kenneth slipped into his gray wool overcoat. He took a twenty-dollar bill out of his wallet and left it on the bar to pay for the one drink that he had ordered but never finished. Joseph and I said nothing to stop him as he walked out of the bar.

15

For the rest of December I watched Judith's house for signs of life. I expected her and Naomi to return from Connecticut at any moment, and so every day I eagerly awaited their arrival. In the morning, on my way to the store, and again at the end of the night, and on occasion during the day, I stared into the house, hoping to see the flutter of a curtain or a passing shadow in the window. Without her and Naomi, the nights were suddenly hard. I found that it was difficult to sleep. I paced around my apartment and stayed up late listening to the BBC's reports on Eastern Europe and the Middle East. I decided it was going to be a bloody, terrible winter. Back at the store I finished reading *The Brothers Karamazov* by myself. I came back to the final pages with Alyosha and the young boys gathered around him, the death of the innocent Illusha adding a certain touching senti- mentality to the scene, which continued to bring a few tears to the corners of my eyes regardless of how often I read it. I read out loud to the shelves and empty aisles my favorite passage:

> People talk to you a great deal about your education, but some good, sacred memory, preserved from childhood, is perhaps the best education. If a man carries many such memories with him into life, he is safe to the end of his days, and if one has only one good memory left in one's heart, even that may sometime be the means of saving us.

I memorized the passage by reciting it on my way to work. I highlighted it in the book for Naomi, knowing even then that it would never make its way back to a shelf. *Remember this*, I wrote in the margins.

I filled in my afternoons by making a list of aphorisms, some new, some borrowed, that I wanted to tell her.

Never trust anyone who says "Trust me."

Try to find high places to look down from.

I wanted to give her a catalogue description of the world, a list of rules by which she could live her life and spare herself the same disappointments that I had already suffered.

On New Year's Eve I sat on a bench in the circle and toasted General Logan with the same stale bottle of scotch Judith and I had shared. I got drunk and then walked home alone. Two days later, I went to pay my rent and found that I barely had enough money to get through the month. Business had steadily slowed down since the neighborhood first began to change, but the last four months had been the quietest since I first opened the store. A month before Judith moved into the neighborhood a single six-story brick housing project that sat on the edge of Logan Circle had been declared uninhabitable and was torn down. At least half the people who lived in it had been regulars at my store, and when the building went, they and their small daily purchases went with it. More dramatic departures had been happening all around me as well, but I had tried hard at first not to give them too much weight. Moving vans were showing up around the neighborhood again, but these were leaving, not coming. They were short and shabby, stacked from the ground to the roof with half-packed boxes of clothes and dishes, mattresses tied in pairs to the roofs. Rents had been on the rise for over a year, but it was only now, in the past six months, that you began to see the effects. Evictions had become common. I often overheard Mrs. Davis standing in front of our house complaining about them and the rent increases. A name or address would float by—

"You know the Harris family."

—and instantly I would turn a deaf ear to the rest of what she had to say.

On the few occasions she had tried to grab my attention, I had simply stood there, mute, nodding my head as need be. She always said the same thing every time.

"It's not right. These people coming in like that and forcing us out."

I was in no position, though, to say what was right or wrong. I was not one of "these people," as Mrs. Davis had just made clear to me. I hadn't forced anyone out, but I had never really been a part of Logan Circle either, at least not in the way Mrs. Davis and most of my customers were. I had snuck into the neighborhood as well. I had used it for its cheap rent, and if others were now doing the same, then what right did I have to deny them? At first I had even believed that the steady stream of new, affluent faces moving into the neighborhood would eventually more than make up for the loss. With the exception, though, of a few things here and there—trash bags, laundry detergent, candy bars, and of course, bottled water—most of these people wanted nothing to do with my little run-down store.

The prostitutes, and the line of cars that came with them, had also thinned out as the neighborhood moved from decay to respectability. I had stopped staying open late; there was almost no one left to cater to. All of that, along with those days in December when I couldn't find the energy or courage to face my store, had taken their toll on what little money I had. Life was precarious. I had always been willing to admit that. I lived on a fine line with poverty on one side and just enough extra money for an occasional beer on the other. In January I slipped off that line, and after that, it was all but impossible to get back on.

☙

"You have to change with the times, Stephanos."

That was Kenneth's advice when I showed him my accounts for November and December. I was never good with numbers. He didn't have the heart to say it, but I knew he was thinking it: it was amazing that I had lasted this long.

"You can't rely on a bunch of kids and prostitutes to make your living anymore. A year from now this could be one of the most exclusive neighborhoods in the city, and you have to be ready for that."

"How?" I asked him.

"By investing. By preparing for the future. You can't stay still, man. You have to move on. That's the way the world works. I've been telling you and Joseph this for years, but you never listen."

It was Kenneth's suggestion that I put a deli counter inside of the store.

"Americans love sandwiches," he said confidently.

I paid for it with a credit-card offer that came in the mail. I ordered the best meat that I couldn't afford and arranged it neatly behind the glass case. I bought a stand-alone chalkboard sign that I placed in front of the store. For the first time, I used the name that Joseph had given me.

Logan's Market
Now Offering Freshly Made Sandwiches to Order!

I began to work longer hours again. I opened the store at six a.m. and closed it at ten on most nights. On the days that I couldn't bear the thought of returning to my apartment, I kept the store open until midnight, hoping, however irrationally, for the remaining trace of the late-night crowds that used to keep my store afloat. At the end of that first week in January, I figured out how much extra I was earning by keeping my store open for four to seven hours longer. The grand total averaged out to twenty dollars a day. I ate sandwiches three to five times a day. Deducting for the food and the extra cost of electricity, I was earning approximately three dollars an hour.

On January 7, I called my mother and brother as soon as I woke up to wish them a merry Christmas. They had received the presents I mailed them.

"What made you think of giving me a book of poems?" my mother asked me.

I told her that the poems in the collection reminded me of her.

"Read the one that begins, 'For each ecstatic instant.' You'll see why."

I told her what I knew about Dickinson, about her lonely, unmarried life in rural Massachusetts and the drawers full of poems found after her death. My mother took the story personally, as she took every story she ever heard.

"*Betam asazinya,*" she said when I finished.

"It is sad. But it's wonderful at the same time." I tried to explain to her the beauty of living such a solitary and lonely life. "She wrote all of those poems entirely alone. She was able to live on just that."

She asked me if I had received the present she had sent me. I was too ashamed to say yes. That money order was the only reason I could afford the phone conversation I was having right then.

"Did Dawit like the shirt?" I asked her instead.

"He loved it," she said. "It fit him perfectly."

I smiled when I heard that. Of course it fit, I wanted to tell her. I already knew exactly what he was made of.

That was the last quiet week in January. The next morning, the only family living in a run-down, three-story house one block away from my store was evicted. An angry crowd gathered outside to watch. The police were called in. From my store I could hear the barrage of shouts and threats volleyed back and forth. More sirens followed, until eventually the entire block was cordoned off. I stepped outside of my store once to see what was happening, but I knew my place. It was behind the counter, not in the middle of a dispute in which I had no part to play.

Less than twenty minutes after the first police car arrived, the entire scene was over. The family had packed up what they wanted and left the rest of their belongings either in the apartment or strewn over the sidewalk and street in a block-long trail of clothes, shattered glass, and worthless paper. The crowd moved on, but no one was ready to surrender quite yet. They slowly worked their way over to my store, where they released some of their long-held frustration in a whir of junk food. I knew every face at least by sight, but at that moment no one acknowledged me or said a word in my direction. When the crowd moved on a few minutes later, my register was fuller than it had been in days.

The next three days saw two more evictions. These were conducted secretly, early in the morning, when no one was around to witness them. The crowd came back nonetheless, a blend of middle-aged and unemployed women, men whose careers depended on the odd jobs they bounced back and forth between, and teenage boys who had nothing better to do than stand around and righteously declare that what was happening was indeed fucked up. The crowd gathered in the circle spontaneously in the aftermath of each eviction and grew larger over the course of the afternoon as people came out of their homes to take part in what was happening. I watched them from my store and waited for them to come in, and they did. People came in waves and bought bags of pork rinds, cans of sweet soda, beer, and plastic-wrapped pickles. I heard rumors of letters that were going to be written, protests that could be staged, and meetings that were being planned. An air of conspiracy was slowly building, and even if it never amounted to more than indignant chatter, there was a sense that something drastic was lying on the horizon.

Those three days were a boon for my little store. It was almost like old times, with my register ringing and a buzz of numbers and voices constantly floating around in my head. I made enough each one of those days to walk home at the end of the night grateful and relieved. America was a beautiful place once again.

I didn't know any of the people who had been evicted, but after the second eviction, I did go out of my way one night to pass by each of their homes to see what they had left behind. It was late enough so no one was around. I took my time and rummaged through the dirty clothes lying on the ground. It didn't matter where you lived, or where you came from, or how far you had traveled, somewhere near you someone was on the run. I pitied and resented those people, whoever they may have been, for being chased out of their homes, perhaps in part because I felt even then a similar fate waiting for me once more.

I kicked a faded white cotton T-shirt with holes near the bottom across a frozen stretch of dead grass, and then turned around and walked back to my apartment.

Ф

A few days after that last eviction, Mrs. Davis came into my store carrying a stack of flyers under her arms. A community meeting was going to be held in a church basement with the neighborhood's councilman. She placed one flyer on the counter and tapped it twice with her finger. I couldn't help but smile as she pushed the flyers toward me. I knew that there were patterns to life, but what I had never understood until then was how insignificant a role we played in creating them.

"We need as many people there as can make it," she said to me.

PROTECT OUR NEIGHBROHOOD
NO MORE EVICTIONS

She had spent all afternoon walking around on her arthritic joints passing around those handwritten, misspelled copies to every friendly store and building she knew. The bottom of the flyer was signed The Logan Circle Community Association. I had never heard of it before. Perhaps it had always existed, but more likely than not, it had been created on the spur of the moment by Mrs. Davis and the other widows of the neighborhood. The name carried a certain natural legitimacy to it, which was important if you ever wanted anyone to believe you.

Mrs. Davis handed me a stack of flyers.

"Here. You can give these out to people when they come in the store."

She caught my smile.

"What's so funny?"

"Nothing," I said. "Of course I'll pass them out."

"And you'll be at the church on Wednesday night."

"Yes. I'll be at the church."

Mrs. Davis took her leave of my store and me with all of the dignity she could have created for herself. She took a carton of milk with her for the road. She drank it by the gallon every week to strengthen her bones and fight her arthritis. I suspected that she washed her face and hands in it as well. Some people grow old passively. Others, like Mrs. Davis, are committed to battling any and every obstacle that approaches them, regardless of how ridiculous or impossible.

I waited until she was safely out of sight before I threw out all of the flyers she had given me.

✤

The Second AME Church was located two blocks south of the circle in the middle of a street that, up until a couple of years ago, was known for the casual ease with which drugs were bought and sold on it. The block still retained more than a few remnants of its old splendor, including two abandoned Victorian mansions that were now being slated for historic preservation. The Second AME Church dated back to the late nineteenth century. A massive gray-brick building that sat on the corner of the block, it had passed through Methodist, Baptist, and Episcopalian hands before being abandoned in the 1950s. For nearly two decades the building sat empty, deteriorating year by year with the Victorian mansions that sat just up the street. Finally, in the 1970s, the building was bought by the AME Church from the city for twenty dollars. Money came in from both liberal and conservative politicians to pay for the new wooden pews, and to fix the broken stained-glass windows and the cracked steps leading up to the church. The congregation swelled through the '70s and early '80s. When I first moved into the neighborhood, my store was packed on Sunday mornings with black women in their elaborate pastel Sunday hats and men in their best and brightest suits. Even after most of them drove back to their homes in the suburbs or in less run-down parts of the city, some of their affluence still seemed to linger in the neighborhood. The foreign crowds began to thin out with the rapid deterioration of an already broken neighborhood. The congregation grew smaller year after year, until the church became what it is today—a meetinghouse for the neighborhood's widows and lonely old men.

The meeting was being held in the church basement, in a room built to hold two hundred people, on one of the coldest nights of the winter so far. At least a hundred folding chairs were set down for the night, neatly split in two halves by a wide aisle large enough for strollers and wheelchairs down the middle. In the corner, right by the entrance, fifty more chairs were stacked on top of one another. There was a fold-up table in the front, with one seat in the center reserved for the neighborhood's city councilman. It was empty as well. I arrived at the meeting twenty minutes late. Not counting Mrs. Davis and four other women who were sitting in the front row, I was the twenty-third person there.

I was counting the heads from the back of the room, noting the familiarity of certain people just by the way they sat in their chairs, or the way they wore their hair tied neatly in a bun or carefully slicked back, when I noticed Judith sitting in a row all by herself in the middle of the room. She was the only white person there. No one had seen me come in, and for a few minutes I considered simply turning around and leaving. All that time I had spent waiting for her to return, and now here she was, exactly where I least needed or wanted her to be.

Had Mrs. Davis not stood up to address the crowd, I would have slipped back out the door and returned to my store, where I could have sat comfortably alone through the night, but she saw me the minute she turned to face the crowd.

I took a seat in the back row by myself.

"I can hardly see you all the way back there, Mr. Stephanos," Mrs. Davis called out.

Besides Naomi, she was the only person I knew who called me Mr. Stephanos. There was something friendly and yet mocking in the way she said it, something akin to the way you can occasionally hear a mother refer to her son as a "big boy."

Judith turned around in response to Mrs. Davis's scolding to see me sitting nervously in the back. I stood up. Judith moved her coat off the seat next to her. Mrs. Davis caught the gesture and followed me with her eyes to see where I was going to sit. It had become that type of meeting. I saw that now. Poor Judith. She didn't know what she had walked in on. All she had seen was a chance to demonstrate her high-minded concern, her belief in participatory democracy and Emersonian ideals.

I took my time gathering my coat and scarf. There were definite sides, and the people in that room were all waiting to see which one I was going to choose.

I smiled warmly at Judith as I passed her row. She turned her head in the opposite direction and threw her coat back over the empty seat. I walked all the way to the front. I took a seat in the first row, on the opposite side of Mrs. Davis and her committee. I focused all of my energy and attention on a flyer posted in front of me for a potluck dinner being held in the church the following week. I read the words over and over—Join Us for a Special Night of Food and Friends—like a prayer that, if said often enough and with the proper conviction, could bring the world to a complete stop.

A dozen more people trickled in behind me, bringing the grand total of people in the room to less than forty. Everyone in that room, with the exception of Judith, had lived in this neighborhood for at least as long as I had. A few of the younger faces in the crowd had still been children when I moved in.

Mrs. Davis began the meeting by thanking everyone for coming. She apologized for the missing councilman, who, according to her, had just phoned to say he had an important meeting with the mayor that was going to run late. She paused briefly after she finished that last sentence—a meeting with the mayor—so we could understand her proximity to the great powers of the city. One of two things was inevitably true: either the councilman had actually called and said what Mrs. Davis had just told us, or he had never been asked to come in the first place. There was a rehearsed and scripted quality to Mrs. Davis's speech that convinced me the latter was true.

"We're all concerned about the direction our neighborhood is moving in," she began. As she spoke she moved quietly, almost imperceptibly, from one side of the room to the other. Her small feet shuffled like sandpaper across the yellow linoleum tile with every word she spoke.

"I can't even begin to count how many old friends I've had to say good-bye to in the past six months. These are people just like you and me. Some of them have been living here their whole lives just to find that one day they can't afford to pay the rent. I don't have to tell you that this isn't right. We all know that. Now it's up to us to figure out what we're going to do about it."

The crowd was more than receptive to everything Mrs. Davis had to say. The last line received a long hum of appreciation that was followed by whispered comments of approval. After a few more words, Mrs. Davis opened the meeting to anyone who wanted to speak. The grievances and frustrations came quickly. Some had to do specifically with the changes in the neighborhood, others were more general and came from a deeper, longer-standing frustration with life. One older man, dressed in a shabby navy blue suit that had grown too large for his body, talked about his wife, who had passed away three years ago, and the children who never came to visit. He said what was happening to the neighborhood wasn't right, but it was impossible to tell anymore where the disappointments of his life ended and those of the neighborhood began. Another woman, young, or at least desperate to seem so, with a black and blond weave that roped down to her waist, complained about her neighbor's boyfriends, who came in and out of the building at all times of the night. As she spoke, she rapped her long plastic nails against the chair in front of her so that each word was punctuated with the click-clacking of her nails on metal. When the speeches came back to the neighborhood, the people's anger was barely disguised. I don't know who used the word "they" first. It might have been Mrs. Davis, or the woman with the blond and black weave who rapped her fingernails and spoke furiously. Once the word entered the meeting, it seemed to trail onto the end of nearly every sentence. I don't know who they think they are. What are they doing here anyway. They have their own neighborhoods and now they want ours too. It's bad enough that they have all the jobs and schools. I was convinced that if given enough space and time, a conclusion would have been drawn that held "them" responsible not only for the evictions in the neighborhood, but for every slight and injury each person in that room had suffered, from the children who never made it past junior high to the unpaid heating bill waiting in a dresser drawer.

Judith sat through the speeches with her legs crossed and her chin resting on her hand. Every time someone spoke I turned around farther than necessary just so I could catch a glimpse of her. She kept tucking and untucking that same strand of hair behind her ear. A few times she caught me watching her. I wanted her to wave or smile at me, but instead she quickly turned her head in another direction, as if she knew that I would have done exactly the same.

She was implicated in every recrimination. No one addressed her directly, but more than a few of the people who spoke that evening turned toward her. Finally Judith raised her hand to speak. It wouldn't have been like her to sit passively through any debate.

She stood up to address the crowd.

"I've only lived in the neighborhood for less than half a year now," she began. "But I share the same concerns as you."

She didn't get any further than that. She paused just long enough in between her sentences for someone in the crowd to yell, "Shut up." She wavered for a second. She gripped the chair in front of her and seemed briefly poised to continue on with whatever she was going to say, but the moment passed. She sat back down and crossed and uncrossed her legs. All eyes, including my own, were still trained on her. Mrs. Davis hurried to resume the meeting by announcing that a petition to the city council had been drawn up. She asked everyone to read it carefully before signing.

> We, the long-time residents of Logan Circle, oppose the further exploitation of our community by developers. We demand that the city council oppose any further development in Logan Circle that jeopardizes the livelihood of the current residents. We demand that the city council investigate the illegal evictions by corrupt landlords.

The petition circulated quickly around the room. No one had to read beyond the first sentence. When the petition reached Judith, she graciously received it and passed it back to the woman sitting a row behind her.

Another meeting was announced for the second week in February. Mrs. Davis assured the crowd that if there were enough signatures on that petition, the mayor himself would be here for that one.

There was no distinct ending point to the meeting that night. People just began to stand and walk around the room as the petition circulated from one hand to the next. Judith gathered together her coat and purse and briskly walked out. No one but me seemed to notice or care. After she left, and everyone in the room except me was standing, Mrs. Davis came over to me and kissed me on the cheek.

"I wish it hadn't gone that way," she said. "That woman's going to go home and think we're a bunch of ignorant fools."

"No, she won't," I told her. "She's better than that."

I left Mrs. Davis with the intention of taking a slow, long walk home around the circle. When I neared my house, though, I saw that Judith's porch light was on. Its warm glow stood out from the harsh streetlights and extended over just barely onto my house. She was sitting on the top of her steps, bundled up in a coat, smoking a cigarette whose smell cut straight through the cold emptiness of the air.

"I thought you had quit smoking a long time ago," I said.

"I did. But sometimes you get lonely and there's no better company in the world."

"I didn't know you were back in town. You should have come by the store and said hi."

"I got in a few days ago, but I've been busy. I've barely been home at all since I got back. Naomi was having such a nice time with my sister and her kids that I didn't want to rush back here. I forget sometimes that she's just a kid."

"Is she already asleep?"

It's funny the gestures we come up with to avoid saying what we already know to be true. Before answering, Judith dutifully extinguished the cigarette into a bowl by her side. She rubbed it into a pulp and then blew the last stream of smoke into the steps. She cast aside a strand of hair that had fallen in front of her face.

"I left her in Connecticut," she said. "I transferred her to a boarding school up there."

I didn't try to hide my disappointment, but even if I had it wouldn't have mattered. It would have shone through anyway.

"She wanted me to give you something."

She stood up and went into her house. I followed her only into the hallway. She came back a second later carrying the large white box with the red bow that Naomi's father had sent her.

"Naomi already opened it," she said. "She wanted to give it to you right away but I wouldn't let her. I didn't think it would be decent. Once we decided she was going to stay in Connecticut I couldn't refuse."

"It's from her father."

"She hardly knows him anymore. And what she's seen, she's not too fond of. According to her, he has bad breath. He met us in Connecticut. I told him about you and Naomi in the store together and he said, 'Fine, let him have it, if that's what she wants.'"

"Does he?" I asked her.

"What?"

"Have bad breath?"

Judith smiled.

"He likes to smoke cigars. He was the perfect academic that way. A terrible husband, but a great economist."

Judith handed me the box. It was heavier and felt more expensive than I had expected.

"Are you going to tell me what it is?"

"Go ahead and open it."

I put the box down on the stairwell and untied the ribbon for the second time in that present's life. Judith had even gone to the trouble of putting new packing paper inside the box.

"It's a typewriter."

"Not just a typewriter," she said. "Look closely at the keys."

Each key was a different animal, and each animal was framed by a different color. I looked closely and counted one animal for every typing finger. There was a bird, a bear, a dog, a duck, a pig, an elephant, a mouse, and a cat. A procession of increasingly large elephants lined the space bar. It was a beautiful typewriter; antique, in perfect condition, solid black with the word "Corona" etched elegantly in gold in the center, and again at the top.

"They made it in the thirties to teach kids how to type. That's what the animals and colors are for. The bird was the pinky finger, the elephants the thumbs. You get the picture."

It was a perfect present for a child like Naomi.

"I don't think I can take this," I said.

"I know. But I promised Naomi that I would at least make the offer. Someday I hope she'll want to look back and remember her father for something more than his bad breath, but she was very fond of you."

There it was again. Judith's use of the word "fond," echoing her "sweet" from a month ago. It was the sensitive, proper word in both cases. Naomi was fond of me, just as she was fond of her stuffed animals and bedroom and some of her teachers. I realized, however touched I might have been by her presence in my life, just what an insignificant role I had played in hers.

"I was fond of her too. She's the only child besides my little brother that I've ever been attached to."

"She wants you to write her at school. I think that's why she wanted you to have this typewriter. It would have obligated you to write her. She said, 'Tell Mr. Stephanos that he has to write me while I'm away.'"

"I would have written her anyway."

"I know. That's what I told her."

We both began to miss Naomi in our own possessive and competitive way, and had I not changed the subject, we could have just stood there awkwardly staring down at that typewriter until we couldn't stand to be near each other.

"I'm sorry about what happened at that meeting," I said.

"Don't apologize," she said. "I know how these things go. You didn't do anything."

She didn't mean it as an attack, but it felt like one anyway.

"I could have said something."

"And what do you think that would have done? If I had lived here as long as they had, I'd be angry too. What I couldn't do was sign that petition. That would have been the definition of hypocrisy, don't you think? I'm embarrassed to say what I paid for this house. Even after all the repairs. I can't pretend that there's anything just to it, but there's nothing evil to it either."

"I saw the new sign in front of your store. It looks good."

"You should come in and have a sandwich. They're the best in the neighborhood. I make my own bread. Slaughter my own deli meat in the basement."

"Sounds tempting."

"Good. Come by tomorrow and see for yourself."

I couldn't hide the eagerness in that last line. I hadn't even known it was there until there was enough space for it to appear.

"Maybe," she said. "I'm sure I'll see you around regardless."

✧

The next day a brick was planted in Judith's car, her white Volkswagen Cabriolet with Virginia license plates and a troop of stuffed animals pressed against the rear window. The brick shattered most of the windshield and landed squarely on the driver's seat. There were flecks of glass all over the interior of the car and sidewalk. They were the first things that caught my eye when I walked out of my house early in the morning to head to work. They sparkled the way I imagined crystals or diamonds would have in the sun.

The other cars—a bright red Monte Carlo sedan with white seats, and a baby-blue Chevy Impala—parked behind and in front of Judith's were untouched. I walked closer to Judith's car so I could peer inside. There was a stack of books still sitting on the passenger seat next to a haphazard pile of CD cases and a few envelopes bearing Judith's name. Whoever threw the brick through the car had no intention of stealing it. All they had wanted was to shatter the windshield, and having done that, were happy to walk away.

I rang Judith's doorbell to tell her what had happened. It was only a few minutes past seven in the morning. The sun had been up for less than a half hour. It was going to be a cloudy, cold day: the definition of a winter morning. The only people out were the new early-morning joggers, who seemed to increase in number by the week. I wondered, briefly, how I could get them into my store before or after their runs.

It wasn't Judith who answered her door that morning. I rang the doorbell at least three times before a sleepy man wearing a long white terrycloth robe answered the door. I saw his figure and his color through the glass. I thought briefly of running away, and had I more time between my first impression of him and his opening of the door, I would have. He had a face like an eagle, a soft brown muddled skin tone that suggested multiple ancestries: part black, part Arab, with perhaps even a touch of the French colonist. This was the face of the celebrated economist who had cigar-tinged breath, lived all over the world, and sent home typewriters to his daughter. A handsome, even beautiful face defined by a long, thin nose and thick, wavy black hair that had streaks of gray so perfectly placed that they could have been artificial.

There was a defensive, guarded look to his face when he opened the door and found me standing on the porch. I knew that look all too well. It was the same one I employed whenever someone entered my store with the obvious intention of begging. Had it been later in the day, he would have tried to shoo me away with a quick flick of his wrist.

"Judith's car," I said, "has been broken into." I said the words with an obviously forced elegance, a touch of Kenneth's fake English accent lurking behind my words, as if what I had really wanted to say from the moment I opened my mouth was, "The tea is ready."

Before the man could respond, Judith's voice appeared from somewhere in the house. It called out: "What is it? Who's down there?"

I had never thought of her voice as being shrill, but at that moment it seemed to be the epitome of the word.

The eagle spoke. It turned its head back slowly to face the steps. It said in French: "There's a man saying your car has been broken into."

Judith ran down the steps. Her first words, the moment she saw that it was me the man had been referring to, were those of an introduction. Her instinct for diplomacy couldn't be matched. For a second she seemed to have completely forgotten why she had come down the steps in the first place, but as soon as she saw me she slowed her steps to a crawl and braced herself. I half-expected her to open her arms and bellow my name from above.

"Sepha, this is Ayad. Ayad, Sepha. He's my next-door neighbor."

She made the introductions casually, as if we were acquaintances meeting at a dinner party being thrown in her honor. Ayad couldn't help but lean out the door to look at the dilapidated buildings on either side of Judith's house for comfort. There was a barely repressed smile behind his face when he faced me again. He seemed to want to apologize for having overestimated me from the beginning.

"I'm terribly sorry to disturb you so early in the morning," I said again in my exalted Cambridge-touched tone. "But I noticed as I was leaving my house that your car had been broken into."

Judith grabbed a long, black wool coat hanging in the hallway and slipped on a pair of worn tennis shoes that could have dated back to her years as a graduate student. They had that soft worn look, the kind that breeds unnecessary, sentimental attachments. She walked down the steps of her house and over to her car. She stared at the shards of glass crunching under her steps. She walked around to the front of her car. As soon as she saw the gaping hole in the windshield, and the brick lying innocently on the seat, she gasped audibly. She held her right hand over her mouth, as if she wanted to cry or scream but had suddenly forgotten how to do either.

Ayad and I watched her from the porch. I wanted him to do something dramatic, something uniquely French, like shrug his shoulders casually and whisper in a raspy voice, *"C'est la vie,"* or pull a cigarette from the pockets of his white robe and smoke with a world-weary indifference. Instead, he just leaned against the doorway and watched Judith mourn her broken car, just as I did.

I walked away from the two of them, touched by the casual, even cruel way they must have treated each other. I walked all the way around the circle to reach my store so I would be less tempted to turn back and see whether Judith was still standing in the street by herself. It didn't work. I turned back anyway, and when I did, I saw that she was still standing there alone, arms folded, as if she had been here and done this before.

There was talk of Judith's car all morning in the store. The police were called in, and inevitably their whirling lights drew a small crowd. I didn't hear any speculation as to who could have done it or why. But still people talked. They said things like: "You know that woman who owns that house on the circle . . . that big red one with all the windows." I realized after overhearing a few of these conversations that what stood out the most, more than Judith and her car, was the house. The formerly rundown, four-story brick mansion that had been abandoned for as long as I had lived here. Look at it now. It was shining. I actually heard someone use that word. That shining big house. There was more than just a sense of mystery to its transformation. There was something that bordered on the miraculous, the impossible. Less than a year ago, no one who lived in this neighborhood would have ever imagined such a feat was possible, but here it was. Mixed in with the pride that inevitably came with living in such close proximity to a house as grand as Judith's was the unshakable faith that there was something not quite right to the whole affair. We expect the things that are dead or dying to remain so. But what happens when they refuse to stay that way?

Business continued to boom and people continued to talk and speculate about what happened. By noon, the brick had moved from Judith's car to her living room. By midafternoon, there was a note attached it to. By four or five in the afternoon, the note had been deciphered. It said: *Get out.* Or: *Move out.* Somehow the event had been transformed. It had grown in weight and stature. It had become political. One drunk old man who lingered around the circle and my store claimed to have seen the whole thing. He reported seeing a group of young men dressed entirely in black throwing the brick through the car or the house (it didn't really matter which anymore) in broad daylight. He said they threw the brick and walked away, cool as ever.

Mrs. Davis made her way into the store near the end of the day.

"I bet you already know what happened to that woman's car," she said to me as soon as she walked in.

"I do," I said. "I was the one who first saw it this morning." (Yes, I was guilty too of wanting to claim my own minor role in what was happening.)

"They towed that car out of there pretty quick. I never even got the chance to see it. What did it look like?"

"It looked like a car that had been broken into."

My answer wasn't enough for her. Perhaps I could have done more to clear the record, but people have to want to know the truth before they can hear it, and who could possibly care for simple facts when the myths being spun did so much more?

The next brick found a home less than twenty-four hours later. This time it wasn't a car but a building. The Hampshire Tower, situated right on the corner of New Hampshire Avenue and 12th Street, just a block and a half away from General Logan and his horse. I knew practically nothing about the building, only that it had been built in the 1920s in the midst of that decade's great economic boom, and that more recently, the bushes surrounding the building were used by prostitutes and their johns for quick late-night ventures. The brick shattered the glass windows of the lobby and landed in a fake potted plant near the elevators. The Hampshire Tower wasn't a particularly nice or expensive building, but that hardly seemed to be the point. What mattered was the repetition, and just as important, the increase in scope, from a car to a building.

After that second brick was thrown I began to hear rumors in my store all afternoon. A Mercedes parked on 13th Street had its tires slashed the same night. There was a note attached to the

Hampshire Tower brick that claimed the shattered windows were payment for an evicted family of six. There were more stories of men dressed entirely in black seen walking past the building late at night with a casual, defiant ease, vigilant and heroic.

I kept my store open until close to midnight that night. Customers came in and out until nearly eleven. For a late January night, the weather was exceptionally mild, even remarkable. Every time the doors to the store were opened, a breeze that seemed better suited to April or May would blow in. Outside of my store was a mixed crowd of old and young men making the most of the temporary reprieve from winter. Fragments of their conversation drifted in and out. I couldn't imagine any of them marching down the middle of the street armed with bricks. We all essentially wanted the same thing, which was to feel that we had a stake in shaping and defining what little part of the world we could claim as our own. Boys even younger than the ones standing outside had fought and killed one another all over Addis for that exact reason, and they were at it again now throughout more of Africa than even Joseph, Kenneth, and I cared to acknowledge. At least here, in America, they had this corner to live their lives as they pleased, and if a few of them took to throwing bricks through windows, then we could not judge them.

When I finally returned home I saw that every light in Judith's house had been turned on. I thought of the Christmas tree in her living room, and then of Gatsby and his corner mansion all lit up. There was no party or music, and as I neared her house, I heard her voice yelling at what must have been close to the top of her lungs. Most of the words were indistinguishable. All I could make out was the profanity: fuck you and so on. Her voice came in and out as she walked through her house cursing away at

Ayad, whose figure I could make out from behind the living-room drapes.

I sat down on the steps outside of my house and listened to them scream and curse at each other. I wondered whether I would catch a glimpse of the rumored black-clad men if I waited there long enough. Anything seemed possible at that point. It was fifty degrees and it was January.

ф

I found a brick in front of my store the next morning. It was lying right in front of the door, as harmless as a fallen branch or leaf. The windows and door to my store had metal grates too thick and close together to have let anything as large as a brick go through them. I checked all the grates and found hardly any signs of damage.

I opened my store as usual. I used the brick that had been given to me to prop the door open. The warm weather had held through the night, and I didn't want to miss any of it.

Judith was my first customer that morning. She came in with heavy bags under her eyes, her hair tied up in a sloppy bun that left loose strands to fall around the sides of her face. She was wearing the same tennis shoes she used to walk to her car that morning, along with a pair of faded jeans and a thick University of Connecticut sweatshirt.

She came in and handed me a letter.

"It's from Naomi," she said. "It came in the mail the morning you stopped by the house. I meant to give it to you that day. And to tell you thank you for coming by and letting me know about the car, but somehow all of that got lost."

She looked up at me and I could see that she wanted some

form of consolation. There was the same shame and embarrassment I had seen in her face when Naomi made her first escape
from the house, and Judith returned to my store to apologize for
her frightened, hysterical behavior. Last night, I had listened to
her and Ayad fight until nearly four in the morning. At some
point they took their fight to the bedroom. I opened my window,
which meant that I could hear nearly everything they said to
each other over the course of the evening. Judith had accused
him of being cruel and indifferent, a self-absorbed asshole who
had used her as a prop to feel better about himself. She told him
that his daughter could barely stand to be around him. She said
that he was ashamed of his own daughter, which made him the
worst possible type of father. Ayad was no less harsh. In a mixture of French and English, he reminded Judith of the role she
had played in seducing him. He told her she was just like all of
the American women he had met: willing and all too eager. Look
at where she was living now, he pointed out. In a shitty slum of a
neighborhood where people throw bricks at your car. He told Judith the only part of his daughter he was ashamed of was the
part that came from her.

There was no address on the envelope. Just my name, properly spelled, in Naomi's elegant, childish handwriting.

"Do you have an address?" I asked her. "There's not one on
this envelope and I'd like to write Naomi back."

Judith pulled a pen out of her pocket and wrote Naomi's address at school on the envelope. Her hand shook with every turn
of the pen.

"Ayad left this morning," she said. "He came back with me
from Connecticut. It was a terrible mistake. One I know never to
make again. I'm sorry you ever had to meet him."

"You don't have to apologize to me," I told her.

"Let's have dinner soon," she said. "Maybe tomorrow if you're free."

Our emotions do get the best of us. Whether they're valid or genuine in the end is irrelevant when all you want is a kind gesture or word to redeem you.

"Yes. Let's do that," I told her.

Judith thanked me for being so sweet and understanding before she left the store. She used those words so easily: "sweet and understanding." She hesitated a moment at the door, but then thought better of whatever else she was going to say. I watched her through the window as she cut through the circle and bounded her way home. I tried to think of what she reminded me of with her quick, long strides somewhere in between a jog and a brisk walk. In the end I decided that it wasn't the way she moved, but the sense of injury that hovered around her that made me think of a wounded animal.

✤

Naomi's letter to me was two pages, front and back, written in purple, blue, and black ink forming carefully scripted letters that were so small I had to hold the paper almost directly in front of my face to read it. Her first few sentences were customary—hi; how are you; I am fine. Every sentence after that was increasingly eloquent. She wrote about her teachers and new friends and the school's "magnificent grounds." She closed by saying that she hoped I wasn't lonely without her. I had always wondered if she was perceptive enough to know how far her presence went toward filling my days. I was relieved to find that she was. She saved the best sentences for last. She wrote them as a couplet:

There are many nice people here, but none as nice as you.
Please write me back, because that's what friends are sup-
posed to do.

I hid the letter under the cash register. I imagined that if I ever wanted to read it again, it would be while I was standing here, behind the counter.

16

There are only three blocks left between General Logan and me. I can just make out the edge of the circle, its empty benches and the trees shaking lightly in the wind. There was a park in Addis that looked just like Logan Circle does from a distance, with a few minor adjustments. That was the other reason I moved into this neighborhood. The first time I saw General Logan riding on his horse, surrounded by his benches and dying clumps of grass, I was reminded of the late-afternoon walks my father and I used to take during the summer, when I spent a part of each afternoon working with him in his office. Near the end of each day he locked up his office doors and together the two of us strolled down the street, past the open-market vendors, through the chaotically jammed roads crowded with cars, buses, and people walking with their small flocks of sheep, everyone fighting for space, until we reached the circle built in the shadows of one of the emperor's palaces. The park was small, no larger than Logan Circle, but it was enough of a reprieve from the city to achieve the intended effect, which was to block out the world in order to live quietly for a half hour or so with our thoughts. My father walked with both hands clasped behind his back and ran silently over the day. Sometimes his thoughts took him even farther back in time, and when they did, he walked around the park talking quietly to himself. He whispered the names of dead relatives—his mother and father, both of whom had died long before I was born. We almost never spoke to each other during those walks. That would have betrayed the lesson he was trying to teach me. It wasn't enough to be comfortable with silence. In order to truly understand it, you had to welcome it and invite it into your life. And so that was what we did. We walked in silence around and around that park until it was time to return to work or home. The last walk we took around that park was on January 23, 1977, less than six months before he was killed. We had just entered the park grounds when we saw the first of seven bodies neatly lined up in the center of the grass. They were lined up in a row, their feet bare, just inside the entrance. They were impossible to miss or avoid. Hung around each of their necks was a crudely made cardboard sign that simply read "Traitor." A lone sentry, no older than the boys lying on the ground, guarded the bodies. He stood to the side so as not to interrupt the view, a rifle slung lazily over his shoulder. It would have been easy enough to turn around and walk back out of the park. With the exception of the guard and the bodies, no one else was there. Instead of leaving, my father pulled me around to his side and placed one arm over my shoulder and led me forward, around the same path that we had always walked on, as if the bodies and the guard assigned to watch them had never been there. It was the simplest act of defiance my father could think of. An arrogant, almost blind refusal to give in to the self-proclaimed terror of the revolution. It was only a few weeks earlier that Mengistu Haile Mariam had declared the start of the Red Terror in a crowded city square by throwing to the ground bottles filled with red ink to represent the blood of the revolution's enemies. And here they were now, lined up like matchsticks on the grass, the soles of their muddy feet exposed to my father and me as we circled the grounds of the park.

Rather than go directly to my store, I turn right at the corner and head toward home. I can see pieces of my store from here. From the corner of 13th and Rhode Island Avenue, I can catch a glimpse of the store's blue and white façade. I can see the outline of my stand-alone chalkboard sign advertising a lunch special that doesn't exist. A turkey and cheddar sandwich on a roll with a complimentary bag of potato chips and a can of soda for $4.50. From here, there is no sign of chaos or destruction. It looks just like any other corner store: humble, well maintained. For a few seconds I imagine that it belongs to someone else. Another immigrant, one who looks much like I do, who right now is standing behind the counter bantering casually with one of his regular customers on a spring day that is all but perfect.

It's almost six o'clock now. The sunlight is hitting the top of the trees. Here is the usual parade of commuters returning home marching around the circle. I find myself walking slowly behind an older black woman dressed far too warmly for the day. She's wearing a heavy, full-length black coat that wraps around her broad, hunched back. She's pushing a red plastic cart in front of her, its contents wrapped in plastic piled to the very top. I walk behind her slowly, admiring the deliberation that seems to come with every step. I can only guess at the effort it takes for a woman like this to make her way through the city every day. I wonder if the world slows down to match her understanding of it, if the mind doesn't catch each passing image and hold it for a second longer in order to compensate for the extra energy each step takes. I wish this day had passed at this pace, that I hadn't run from one end of the city to the other. Despite how hard I may have tried, there is still so much I missed. I should have visited the market by my uncle's house and talked to the old Somali man who used to sell me *injera* and *berbere* when I was still a teenager. I should have taken the time to stand outside of the Capitol Hotel's palatial entrance and marvel at the disappearance of time.

The woman and I part ways in front of what remains of Judith's old house. On the night of the fire, Joseph, Kenneth, and I were sitting in my store. The three of us were sitting around our table eating turkey sandwiches and drinking a cheap bottle of wine Joseph had stolen from his restaurant. I remember I was telling them about what had been happening, beginning with the brick that had been thrown through Judith's car. I told them about Ayad and his eaglelike face, and the rumors of marauding men in black touring through the neighborhood.

Kenneth shook his head in disappointment when he heard the news.

"None of this will be good for business," he had said. "Having bricks thrown through windows is a bad sign."

I told him that business had been better the past week than it had been in months.

"That's just temporary," he said. "Things always go up in times of crisis. People get confused, scared. So what do they do? They spend. If this keeps up, a few weeks from now and this place will be empty."

"It's already empty," I reminded him.

"Well. It will be even emptier."

"This is how it happened in Zaire," Joseph said. "One day we heard that some people were beaten up by guys with guns. The next day we had a rebel group walking through the neighborhood saying they had come to liberate us from the government. To prove their point they shot five people in the street who were responsible for our oppression."

"You must have been grateful," I said.

"Of course we were. We didn't even know that we were oppressed. Imagine our surprise and joy to find out that we had been. We gave the rebels all the money we had to thank them. I remember one man was so happy he even gave them his wife and daughter. As an African, you should understand what's happening here, Stephanos."

"And what is that?" Kenneth asked him.

"That there's nothing these people can do. Look at this place. All of the marches in the world won't change anything anymore. We were at our best in the sixties. Africa was free. America was free. Everyone was marching to something. And now look at us."

I walked over to the door then and picked up the brick that had been thrown at my store that morning. I had left it lying on the ground in case the weather turned nice again.

"I found this in front of my store today," I said.

Joseph took the brick from my hand and turned it over and over as if he were checking its density and weight. He paused and held it in his lap silently as he thought about what he was going to say next. He wanted to say something important, something worthy of a brick left lying on a doorstep.

"There's a great metaphor in this," he said. He held the brick in the air with one hand. It could have been a poem from Yeats that he was talking about for all of the import and dignity he was

attributing to the brick. His words and gestures were borrowed—
part academic, part statesman. They were all wrong. Watching
him, I couldn't help but think that in Africa, he could have led a
crowd straight to the bush or palace. He had that kind of
charisma about him when he spoke.

"The Palestinians have their rocks. The Rwandans had their
machetes. Our weapons aren't accidents," he said. "They're a
part of who we are."

"It's just a brick, Joseph," Kenneth said.

"That's exactly my point," Joseph responded.

After that we began to catalogue the child wars fought over
the last three decades when the roar of the fire trucks and ambulances caught us in midthought. Kenneth was pressing his case
that every war in Africa was essentially a war fought by and
against children. He was asking us to look at the numbers, at the
sum total of children's lives lost in battle, and just as important,
the even greater number lost in the margins of those battles. He
was saying, "It's a simple matter of arithmetic. You can't deny
the numbers," when I noticed that the sirens and the lights that
accompanied them had come to a halt on the other side of the
circle. The store was spinning in red and white. Kenneth's voice
was being drowned out by the hard-pressed wailing sound coming from another fire truck that was rounding the corner. His
voice trailed off as the three of us looked up from the table and
out the window into the indiscriminate glare of the emergency
lights twirling like a disco ball around the circle. We have instincts for tragedies. We know when they belong to us long before we understand them. Even before I ran out of the store,
across the circle, to the wall of waiting fire trucks, ambulances,
and police cars, parked in front of my house, I knew.

This is how it began, then, with the three of us sitting in my store on a Thursday night listing for the hundredth time the victims of a continent that at times seemed full of nothing else. We were always more comfortable with the world's tragedies than our own. That night was no different. Coups, child soldiers, famines were all a part of the same package of unending grief that we picked our way through in order to avoid our own frustrations and disappointments with life. It was only inevitable that the two would have to meet at some point.

The windows to Judith's house are still boarded up, and you can still see streaks of black around the top. The only part of the house not ruined by the fire is the stone steps leading up to the front door. The last conversation I had with Judith was on these steps. It was almost a month ago to the day, on an early April afternoon touched intermittently with a light, cold drizzle. On the night of the fire, she had been off watching a movie and having dinner with her former colleagues. She didn't come back home until the last traces of the fire had died down. The front door, and every window in the house, had been broken. Firefighters and a crowd that had come out to watch the spectacle circled the house. When Judith arrived, I was standing directly across the street with Kenneth and Joseph, surrounded on either side by my neighbors, all of whom had run out of their homes. Even before I saw her I already knew she wasn't in the house. A policeman had told me the moment I approached my building. He said they found the place abandoned when they arrived, and so there had been nothing to do at the time besides stand there and watch the flames burst through the top-floor windows and tear down the molding that lined the roof. Joseph and Kenneth stood close to me as we watched the spectacle and the quickly gathering crowd. The old widows were craning their heads out of their windows, while women and children gathered on the porches, watching safely from a distance. The last time I had seen anything similar was five years ago, when a man was shot and killed in front of General Logan. The line of police cars surrounding the circle had brought out the entire neighborhood then, too.

It was clear from nearly the beginning that my house was going to be spared, as were all of the others surrounding Judith's. If there was a theme to the conversations I overheard, it was: Thank God it isn't us. Grateful, once again, in the way only other people's suffering can make us.

When Judith finally arrived to reclaim what was left of her home, there was a simple, almost casual pragmatism that governed her actions. It was as if she had known all along that her time in Logan Circle was only temporary, despite how hard she may have wanted to believe otherwise. That night we exchanged only a few brief, customary words. I told her how sorry I was, and she accepted my apology with as much conviction as she could muster. I think I realized she was already gone. Logan Circle, her beautiful four-story mansion. She began to leave it all behind the moment she saw the firemen walking nonchalantly out the front door. The whole thing could be shaken off as a protracted bad dream, one that had lasted, from start to finish, approximately five months.

After a brief hug, I left her alone to deal with the firemen and police. Joseph, Kenneth, and I returned to the store.

"So that's her?" Joseph asked me once we were situated around the table once again.

I nodded my head. It would have been too much to have said yes, affirmatively, as if I had ever really known who Judith was.

Back at the store that night, we joined the rest of the neighborhood in speculating as to whether or not the fire had been an accident. There were the lingering questions provoked by the bricks that had been thrown through Judith's car and the Hampshire Tower. But those were minor, perhaps even irrelevant, when compared to the sight of Judith's four-story mansion lit in flames. Joseph insisted that they weren't.

"Everything is connected," he said. "The bricks, this fire. They're not just accidents, Stephanos. That's the way these things begin. With a handful of small actions that build and build. A month from now you could be looking at an entirely new neighborhood."

In the end, nothing changed, Joseph, as grand an event as it may have seemed to you at the time. It was only one desperate, lonely man, not a marauding group, who threw the bricks and set fire to Judith's home. His name was Franklin Henry Thomas, and according to the brief article on him in the *Washington Post*, he had been, until one month earlier, a lifelong resident of Logan Circle. Born just a few blocks away from my store, Frank, as he was known, had lived in the Hampshire Tower for eighteen years with a wife and two children. He worked odd jobs around the neighborhood and city as a handyman. In the summertime, he rode a bicycle around the city offering illegal cable television connections to people on the street. I remember him, but I can't say that I ever knew him or spoke to him. I used to see him riding his bicycle down the street with a book bag strapped around his chest, his middle-aged body far too large for the child's bike he was riding. Occasionally I heard him call out to people sitting on their porches, or standing near their houses, in a high-pitched, singsong voice, "Got cable?" I remember he never paused after he said that, but would continue on down the middle of the street, his oversize body comically cramped onto the seat of his bike, his words left to echo behind him as he zigzagged his way down the road. He was a man who made his living simply hawking whatever meager wares he had.

According to the article, Franklin Henry Thomas lost his one-bedroom apartment in the Hampshire Tower when his lease expired in December and he was asked by his landlord to start paying nearly a third more than he had previously. In February he moved into a temporary shelter while his wife and children moved into an apartment in Maryland with his wife's sister. There was a photograph of him next to the article, one that I clipped out and taped to the side of my register so that at almost any given point in the day, I could turn my head and catch at least a glimpse of the man who had burned down Judith's home. In the picture, Franklin Henry Thomas is bald with an unkempt white beard that looks newly acquired. I was surprised, when I first saw the picture, how closely he and I resembled each other. We had the same narrow face and broad forehead. Had I lost all of my hair and grown a beard, and aged perhaps just a few more years, we could have passed for brothers. Inside my store, with no one around, I said his name often to myself. Franklin Henry Thomas. Franklin Henry Thomas. Sometimes just Frank, sometimes Frank Henry. The name was so decidedly American, so quintessentially colonial in its rhythm and grandeur. I began to think of Franklin Henry Thomas as my coconspirator in life. I even thought briefly of visiting him in jail so I could tell him that I alone understood why he did what he did. He was arrested after the police caught him trying to break into Judith's old house a week after the fire. He was carrying all of his belongings with him in a black duffel bag. Apparently, he had planned on moving into the burned-out building for the remainder of the winter. In his delusion, he had even begun to imagine that perhaps, with a little time, he could repair the house he had burned down and move his family back in with him. His duffel bag was full of the tools he had used as a handyman. He told the police in his confession that he had made sure no one was home when he lit the book of matches that started it all.

After the fire, a police car was parked permanently in Logan Circle. It sat right next to General Logan and his horse. Together, the two stood guard over the neighborhood day and night. Following Frank's arrest, the marauding men in black returned to the corners of the imagination that had created them, and eventually the police car disappeared as well. General Logan was left all to himself once again. As for Judith's house, boarded up now with yellow police tape across the front door, it had returned to a state similar to the one she had found it in. I noticed that no one stopped to look at the house anymore. It was no longer beautiful. It no longer shone. I wonder even now if most of the people who live here don't miss it. There was something nice to living in the shadows of a house like Judith's. There are still pieces from the roof's molding lying on the ground around me, and though the house is now abandoned and desolate in its appearance, there is enough evidence to remember that it wasn't always this way.

From the steps, I can see across the circle, straight to the store. The front door is still open. It's still too early in the evening for a crowd, but soon enough, one will settle onto the corner, regardless of whether the store is open or not. If I had to choose only one thing about the neighborhood that I would never want to see change, this would be it. There's a safety in numbers that goes beyond any home. I've learned this only recently. It's true that after the fire I opened and closed my store sporadically. But it was never because I wanted to see it close, as Kenneth had supposed, or because I wanted to lose whatever customers I still had. In the only letter I ever wrote to Naomi after the fire, I tried to explain what was happening. I tried to tell her that there wasn't much point in holding on to a store, in holding on to anything, if in the end it didn't matter to at least one other person than yourself. "You're right," I wrote. "I do indeed miss having you around the store. It's hard to go back there every day now that I know you and your mother will never return. I can't seem to find any reason to open it up in the morning."

Of course I never mailed that letter. It reminded me far too much of the ones my uncle used to write. I still have it sitting under the cash register next to the letter she had sent me.

Judith never brought Naomi back to see what had become of their house. Perhaps she thought it would have been too tragic a scene for her daughter to witness. In her last visit back to the neighborhood, she took the time to stop by the store to say something resembling a good-bye. I closed the store for the afternoon so the two of us could take a walk back to the house. She said she didn't want to see it alone again. We sat here on these steps in a mixture of sporadic sun and rain and talked about what Judith was going to do next. Of course I suggested that she rebuild, even if I never expected that she would.

"It'd be too much," she said. "To go through all of that work again. It would feel like I was stuck in the past and I don't want to live my life that way. It's better just to start over."

I quoted to her a line from *Democracy in America*, one of a series that she had used as an epigraph to her own book:

"Among democratic nations new families are constantly springing up, others are constantly falling away, and all that remain change their condition; the woof of time is every instant broken and the track of generations effaced."

"That's one of my favorite quotes from him," she said.

"I know."

I didn't have to add that it was because I had read her book.

"I still owe you a dinner," she said. "Maybe once I settle into a temporary place, you can come over and join Naomi and me."

That we haven't spoken or seen each other since then is no surprise. It was enough to pretend, for just that afternoon, that our lives might intersect again.

What was it my father used to say? A bird stuck between two branches gets bitten on both wings. I would like to add my own saying to the list now, Father: a man stuck between two worlds lives and dies alone. I have dangled and been suspended long enough.

There are approximately 883 steps between these steps and my store. A distance that I can sprint in less than ten seconds, walk in under a minute. It is always the first and last steps that are the hardest to take. We walk away and try not to turn back, or we stand just outside the gates, terrified to find what's waiting for us now that we've returned. In between, we stumble blindly from one place and life to the next. We try to do the best we can. There are moments like this, however, when we are neither coming nor going, and all we have to do is sit and look back on the life we have made. Right now, I'm convinced that my store looks more perfect than ever before. I can see it exactly as I have always wanted to see it. Through the canopy of trees that line the walkway cutting through the middle of the circle is a store, one that is neither broken nor perfect, one that, regardless of everything, I'm happy to claim as entirely my own.

ABOUT THE AUTHOR

Dinaw Mengestu was born in Addis Ababa, Ethiopia, in 1978. In 1980, he immigrated to the United States with his mother and sister, joining his father, who had fled Ethiopia during the Red Terror. He is a graduate of Georgetown University and Columbia University's MFA program in fiction and the recipient of a 2006 fellowship in fiction from the New York Foundation for the Arts. He lives in New York City.